Today I Am Going to Die: Choices in Life

"The Awakening Tetralogy" - A Series of Four Spiritual Books, Volume 1

Ken Luball

Published by Ken Luball, 2022.

TODAY I AM GOING TO DIE: CHOICES IN LIFE

First edition. June 1, 2022.

Copyright © 2022 Ken Luball.

ISBN: 979-8985812800

Written by Ken Luball.

Today I Am Going To Die

Choices in Life

A SPIRITUAL BOOK BY

Ken Luball

Author's Note:

My hope writing '*Today I Am Going to Die*', book 1 in *The Awakening Tetralogy,* was to try to awaken and help others who are awakened more fully understand what enlightenment is so their journey through life may be more fully realized.

This book was written with the help of Bodhi, my spirit guide. He is able to easily communicate with me as I write down his thoughts. Though my journey toward enlightenment is not yet complete, Bodhi, being a spirit guide, most certainly is enlightened.

Though '*Today I Am Going to Die: Choices in Life*' is considered fiction, I would like you to imagine, since Bodhi was both my and Rue's, the protagonist in this book, spirit guide, perhaps the story being told may not be fiction, but genuine. Since this story was told to me by Bodhi, about his experiences being a spirit guide previously to Rue, I think the possibility everything he is saying, and the messages he is trying to convey are genuine, and this story may be true.

As you prepare to begin your search for meaning, do so with an open heart and mind, ready to delve deeper into the mysteries of existence. Let us embark on this spiritual adventure together, beginning with the first of this four book series of spiritual novels, and, in doing so, discover the answers you are searching for.

~ ~

Table of Contents

Prologue: The End of Life

After we have lived our lives, as we approach death, it is common to reexamine how our life went. Did we live a successful life? The end of life offers a unique opportunity to do this, because at this time, the ego, our learned self-centered beliefs, loosens its influence on us, And the spirit becomes our predominant reviewer.

At this point in the cycle of life, it no longer matters how much money we made, the size of the house we lived in, the job we had, or anything else associated with success, as dictated in the world by the ego. We are all finally equal now and we judge our success through a different prism: that of the spirit. When we review our lives, what we had thought was success often holds a different meaning now.

It is at this time, especially during the last few days of our life, we come to the realization what we thought was important, really was not. All the material things we accumulated, friends we had, places we visited, jobs we worked, amount of money we made, or any other comparison you can think of, which belongs in the world in which we had lived, becomes meaningless.

It is at that moment, the moment where the ego has minimal control over our actions and decisions, the true meaning of life finally becomes evident. It is then, despite how strongly the ego may have influenced our life before, the opportunity To view our life in a different way presents itself. At this time in our life, primarily viewing our lives through the eyes of our spirit, we may find we have many regrets.

We begin to understand the selfish pleasures in the world we had sought were not very important. As death becomes evident, we finally realize none of that matters. When we die, unless our culture is like that of the ancient Egyptians, our body will be buried or cremated, And nothing we accumulated during our lifetime will accompany us. Our body will then be placed in a coffin or urn, just like every other person who dies, regardless of their stature or their lifetime accomplishments.

At that moment, just before we die, we finally understand we truly are all equal. No one was ever better than another. Race, money, prestige, no longer matter. As we get closer to our death, it becomes evident the self-centered path the ego had us follow to find success and happiness may have not been the right path after all. The fear, hatred, and prejudice we once felt are no longer important to us, not because we are going to die, but because it never did matter.

~ Chapter 1 ~
Choices in Life

A
s I lie here waiting for death, I am alone except for a voice I am clearly able to hear now. It is the voice of my spirit guide, and he has a lot to tell me before the day is over. Everything he is telling me makes complete sense to me now. I wonder why it took so long for me to hear him. What he is saying is so obvious, yet I never understood or heard any of his advice before today. I am disappointed I could not have more time to live or be allowed a do-over in life, knowing what I do today. For if I could, I would have done many things differently.

Instead, I have decided to write this book today, just before I die, so you will hopefully understand the simple message my spirit guide shared with me. It is my hope you will not have to wait as long as I did to make changes in your life, so you will be able to lead a happier, more fulfilling life than I did.

It is heartbreaking to see how many people are as depressed and unhappy as I was, and how easy it is for them to change this. It does not have to take an entire lifetime to make this change; you do not have to wait, as I did, until the last day of your life. In fact, it can be done almost instantaneously. All it takes is the will to make the change and the understanding of the change that is needed.

This book is actually dictated to me by my spirit guide, who spoke to me on the last day of my life. You will be amazed how simple the message is and surprised when you hear and finally understand it.

My name is Rue, which is a traditional English name, literally meaning regret. I am 85 years old now and today is the day I am going to die. I have had a very successful life, a family, three children, four marriages and owned many expensive and glamorous things. I was a famous actress, made a lot of movies, tons of money, knew hundreds of people, and had fans everywhere who adored me. I was also gorgeous: brunette, blue eyes, and a great figure. I knew I was sexy, and I could get anything I wanted in life because of my looks and money.

Today, on the final day of my life, something strange is happening. I must be hallucinating because I can hear a voice I have seldom heard before; it is coming from inside me. This voice is telling me the story of my life. The story begins when I was a baby inside my mother's womb. I thought everything would end today, the day I am to die; I was to discover, though, death is not the end.

I wish the voice would be quiet, but it will not. This voice even has a name. His name is Bodhi and unbeknownst to me, he has been with me my entire life, even before I was born. Bodhi is my spirit guide. He told me I also have another guide that has been with me throughout my life as well; her name is Anatta. Anatta is the word Buddha used to describe what is commonly referred to as the self or ego. Anatta is only present while we are alive, born when we take our first breath and dying, along with our own bodies, when we have taken our last breath. Bodhi, as I was to find out, is eternal.

This is the story of my very successful life as told to me by my spirit guide, Bodhi, on the last day of my life. After I was born, it was difficult to clearly hear Bodhi's voice again. Though I had sensed he may have been there, I was so busy living my life, I never paid much attention to him.

Mine is story of regrets. Though I was famous, wealthy, had a family and knew many people, I really lived a very lonely, superficial life. I was divorced four times and estranged from my three children; I was never there for them while they were growing up or when they were adults and had their own families.

I was so wrapped up living and enjoying my life I did not have very much time left to spend with them. I was always too busy working, traveling, partying, and doing all the things that would make me happy. I gave my children plenty though. They had nice clothes, a big house to live in, a swimming pool, and almost anything else they wanted, if they did not ask for too much of my time. I was also too busy to read them stories when they were little, go to any sporting games, or help them with their homework.

I hired a nanny to take care of those things and a housekeeper to cook for them and keep the house clean. My job was to make money so they could have the best things in life. I was not even home enough for them to get to know me since my life was so busy. I did not understand why they did not like me, since I had given them everything they needed and more while they were growing up.

Though Bodhi is telling this story, the story I am about to tell you is mostly about my other guide, Anatta, who dominated and controlled my life since the day I was born. It was not until today, the day I am going to die, I could finally clearly hear Bodhi's voice again. My story really begins before I was born, when I was inside my mother's womb, and before Anatta joined Bodhi as one of my two guides through life.

Bodhi told me they were like siblings who would fight often after I was born, mostly about trying to tell me the right thing to do. Though they were very different from each other, they would both be important in helping me navigate through life. It would be up to me, though, to determine which to listen to. While Bodhi was very wise, compassionate, empathetic, and loving, Anatta would teach me what I must do to survive in the world. She told me how to act, what the difference between right and wrong and good and bad was, how to get along with other people, and what was important to know so I could be happy.

Anatta was to be my guide through life. She is known by many names; ego, self, psyche, and personality are just four of the names she has. Anatta is my human-self. Among her many traits are self-conceit, self-importance, self-interest, and selfishness. Anatta was to teach me how I should be and act throughout my life, so I could be happy. Unlike, Bodhi, who would be concerned for what was best for everyone, Anatta's only concern was for me. Bodhi gave unconditional love, while Anatta encouraged self-love.

It sounded confusing to me, but I figured I would have a lot of time to sort everything out. After I was born, I knew I would live for 85 years, meet many others who also had a spirit guide and Anatta accompanying them, and have many adventures throughout my life. The outline for my life had been predetermined; some would say my destiny or fate had already been decided, though I would have many choices and paths I could take to get there. The choice of whether to choose the spirit's path of unconditional love or Anatta's path of self-love was mine to make.

If I chose Anatta's path, I would find happiness in the world. More specifically, I would find what I came to believe was happiness. If, however, I would follow Bodhi's guidance while I was alive, the lessons would be much more satisfying and important. Bodhi told me, though I would get to choose who to follow, I would struggle to remember any of what he told me after I was born. He also said he would try to help guide me while I was alive, though I would have to make my own choices throughout my life.

This book is really about our choices in life, which help us decide which of the two paths we will follow. The first, that of Anatta, is the learned path we are taught as we grow up and are socialized. This path allows us to survive in the world. It is the path of the I or self. When we follow this path, our concern is primarily for ourselves, our individual success and happiness in the world. We look for our happiness and love in the world around us and believe a successful life will be defined by money, love, prestige, material possessions, and many other things society convinces us defines success.

The other path we may follow is that of our spirit. Success, by its definition, has to do with sharing our unconditional love present within each of us with all others. According to Bodhi, success and happiness may never be found in the world or through being with another person; it may only be found within, where the spirit is, and then shared selflessly with others. It is here the answers to life are and have always been. By seeking happiness and meaning anywhere else, Bodhi cautions, the result will be confusion, fear, depression, and anxiety.

The constant struggle, as I was to discover, between Anatta and our spirit, defines our very existence and whether we will be able to find meaning and true happiness during our lives. By following Anatta's path through life, as I and so many others do, we are destined to lead an artificial, meaningless, lonely life. To follow Bodhi's path, however, is to follow the intrinsic beliefs and values we are all born with. Bodhi's path is the path of unconditional love, love given without expectation of getting anything in return. Instead of defining success as Anatta would, as I or the self, life is defined as we. Bodhi's belief of success is if everyone succeeds, not just our individual success.

This book is about how we define success and happiness. The choices presented to us may seem black and white, but I assure you they are not. The right path is often difficult to find and, even if you are lucky enough to find it, it is quite easy to be led astray and back onto the other path. Life has a way of putting up barriers as we pursue our desire to find our higher-self.

Whether the problems are personal, financial or anything else, we are often dragged back to the realities of living in a world dominated by fear when they occur. Though I was not lucky enough to find the right path before today, I know many people had tried and, at least temporarily, succeeded. It never seemed very long, though, before stress or a tragedy in their life returned them to the everyday struggles we all experience living in the world.

It takes courage to follow your spirit's path; to do so, you must confront and challenge your past. You must also be willing to take a chance by changing the path you are on and the direction your life is taking. It is important for you to know, though, you will not be giving up your individuality or ability to choose the life you want if you do so.

It is simply easier to continue and not even try, as I did, allowing life to happen to you. The drugs and alcohol I took every day, often beginning early in the morning and ending shortly before I went to bed, allowed me to ignore any feelings or doubts I had. Also, like many others I know, I kept extremely busy so I would not have free time to think about any of this. I justified how much I worked, convincing myself it was necessary because I needed money to buy the many material things and do all the things that would make me happy.

Today, though, I understand the real reason I kept busy was so I would not have enough time to think and confront my problems and past. By staying busy, I also did not have enough time to hear Bodhi. I, therefore, was able to easily ignore the discomfort that arose within me any time I sensed a hint something was wrong.

I do not think I am much different than many others. Many of us are afraid to confront our demons; it is easier to accept the reality of life as it is and bury our feelings and real emotions within. I write this book, on the last day of my life, hoping you may see the many poor choices I made throughout my life, so you may choose a different path through your own life.

Choices in Life

There may come a time in our life we approach a fork in the road. If we take the straighter less challenging road, we may become successful, have money, material possessions, a family, and other symbols a thriving life enjoys, as we approach death, we may find our life has been lived without purpose or meaning.

If, however, we take the sharper curve at the fork in the road, pursuing a more difficult path through life, though the turn is much more challenging, its path quite curvaceous and demanding, it will lead to a genuine understanding about our life's purpose.

Chapter 2
The Meaning of Life

L et me formally introduce myself to you. My name is Bodhi; I am a spirit guide. I am about to tell you a story I am certain you have never heard before; it is the story of my journey through life. Before I tell you, however, perhaps I should tell you what a spirit guide is.

Within everything alive, there is a spirit guide accompanying it throughout its life. Perhaps to try to understand my story better, I will tell you about my last journey through life, one where I accompanied a girl named Rue through her life. The story begins even before Rue was conceived; it actually begins in what you might call the afterlife.

The afterlife is where spirits exist together; some might call it heaven. It is ethereal, existing at a higher vibrational level than on earth. The afterlife is an exquisite beautiful spiritual plane where unconditional love and peace permeate every corner of the realm. It is here we wait until we are asked to accompany a new life through its journey. It is a great honor to join with a new life and I looked forward to accompanying Rue. I know you must be interested in what the afterlife is like; I promise you I will talk about it in much more detail later in my story.

Our story, the story of Rue and I, began in her mother's womb, just after she was conceived. Life begins at that precious moment, and it is there I met Rue for the first time. Inside her mother, it is quiet, dark, and peaceful, and the only emotion I can sense is love. It is a love I was to try to share with Rue after she was born; but as you will soon discover, everything becomes much more complicated after we are born.

At that moment though, my job was to teach Rue about the meaning of life. After she was born, due to the chaos she would be exposed to in the world, I knew my voice would be muted and it would be much more difficult for her to hear me. For after she was born, another guide, Anatta, who is the self or ego, would be born as well. Anatta represents everything we learn while we are alive, and unlike me, who is eternal, Anatta will die at the end of Rue's life, along with the shell they had lived in. After her birth, I would have to compete with Anatta for Rue's attention, in order to help direct her along the spiritual path we are all meant to pursue while we are alive.

If I could teach Rue enough though, while she was growing within her mother's womb and before Anatta was born, then hopefully, her journey through life would not be as challenging. Though it sounds like it would be a difficult task, it really was not. Without the confusion Anatta was to cause after Rue was born, the lessons would not be hard for her to understand.

In order to try to make things easier for you, the reader, imagine Anatta lives within the body and mind of everything that has life after we are born and I, Bodhi, live within the heart. If you can visualize this, I think it may be easier to understand my story.

The meaning of life is not difficult to understand. It is to share the unconditional love existing within our heart with all living things. Life is not meant to be lived in isolation; rather it is meant to be shared with all others, in which a spirit also lives. By sharing this love selflessly, each of us becomes stronger and our journey through life becomes less challenging and more meaningful.

It must be hard to believe it is so simple. Though we are born with this knowledge, the difficult and challenging thing is to remember it after our birth. To simplify this even further, the meaning of life is to return to the knowledge we each are born with before we are exposed to the noise and chaos of the world. Though this may sound easy, nothing could be further from the truth. For after Rue and Anatta were born, my voice was quieted, as Rue was socialized, learning how to survive in the world. Every interaction she had after she was born would further confuse and alter the true path she was meant to take. But I, her spirit guide, am there to help her remember what she once knew, and by doing so, help her return to the spiritual path she was meant to follow through life; to return to the path I was sent to teach her.

We know all the answers, the meaning of life, before we are born. It is only after our birth we forget what we once knew, as it is buried deep within our heart. It is ironic; after we are born, we spend the rest of our lives simply trying to remember this, returning to the path in life we once knew, understood, and are meant to pursue. Instead, we seek out our answers in the world around us, where they may never be found, and leading to many of the problems experienced throughout the world.

The Simple Message We Are Here to Learn

Greed, prejudice, inequity; war, hunger, homelessness. None of these things and so much more need exist today. Every man-made problem and harmful emotion results from accepting the self-centered status quo, the belief we are better and more deserving than another; we are not.

We are all spirit, each with a piece of god within, intimately linked to each other. Every life, therefore, regardless of our differences, is equally important, each deserving to be helped in their time of need and treated with respect and unconditional love. This is the simple message we are here to learn.

Chapter 3
Before I was Born

I t is warm, quiet, and dark. I am inside my mother's womb as I am waiting to be born. I am safe here and feel the unconditional love from my mother. Bodhi is here with me as well; he is telling me he will be with me throughout my life. Bodhi is wonderful; I feel safe as he tries to prepare me for what to expect after I am born. Inside my mother's womb, I feel only joy, happiness, love, and so many other warm comforting feelings. I am excited to be able to see the world, but I must wait until I grow big enough. While I am waiting to be born, Bodhi is telling me about himself and how he will be there to help me during my life. This is the story Bodhi told me as I patiently waited to see the world.

Bodhi is my spirit guide, and he will live, metaphorically, within my heart. A spirit guide is present in all living things, including people, animals, plants, and even the stars and the universe itself. They are eternal and will not only be with me while I am waiting to be born but will also be there while I am alive and after I die as well.

Bodhi, and all other spirit guides, have been known by many names; god, essence, soul, spirit, and higher-self are just five of many others. To not confuse me, he told me it did not matter what I called him; he was simply there to guide me as I lived my life. Bodhi was to exist within my heart and represents unconditional love, which is love given selflessly, without expectation of getting anything in return. He told me to live a successful, happy, and meaningful life, I would need to share this love with everyone and everything alive as well. The goal of life, the reason we are alive, is to join with others in which a spirit is also present and share our love selflessly. By doing so, we learn the true meaning of life. Only by sharing the knowledge and unconditional love of our spirit, by being compassionate, empathetic, and caring, will we all succeed in life. The more we selflessly help each other, the more fulfilling, meaningful, and successful our life will be. I knew I would never be alone since Bodhi would always be with me. I also understood I would be sharing my life with others who also have spirit guides as well, and together, we would spread joy, peace, compassion, and love throughout the world.

Life was wonderful within my mother's womb; it was a good thing I was there for a while, since Bodhi had much to teach me. He taught me why we are born; it is to learn as we experience life. We are supposed to learn the importance of all life, working together, compassion, love, empathy, selflessness, and much more. He explained only by accepting his guidance and sharing this knowledge and love with all others will we be able to answer the questions we have about life. As we come together with other spirit guides, we become stronger, helping each other through life. Our goal is to become one with our spirit, our higher-self and to share the unconditional love and selfless beliefs we have with all others. Bodhi told me we are all equal; no one life is better or more important than another. It would not matter what we looked like, our beliefs, gender, or anything else. All life is precious, for a spirit guide was within them and within everything alive as well. By following the spiritual path through life, we will be able to experience life as it was meant to be.

Bodhi also told me I would be challenged to remember this after I was born. For after my birth, another guide, Anatta, my ego guide or self, would join me through my life's journey as well. Anatta, unlike Bodhi who is eternal, is only present while we are alive. Bodhi explained Anatta represents everything I will learn in the world throughout my life after I am born. Though I did not know what to expect, I was excited to meet Anatta, because I wanted to learn as much as I could.

The more Bodhi taught me, the more I understood everything. Life seemed so simple. All I needed to do was spread Bodhi's selflessness and unconditional love with others. After I was born, if I needed advice or got confused, I only needed to ask, and Bodhi would help me find the right path again.

I knew I would never be alone, for not only was Bodhi going to be with me, but there would be a spirit guide within others who would help me as well. Bodhi tried to prepare me for what life may be like after I left the safety and comfort of my mother's womb, but it did not seem necessary; everything made complete sense. I already had the answers to all the questions about life we want to know after we are born. It was hard to understand how anything could go wrong. To find Bodhi after I was born, all I needed to do was close my eyes, quiet my mind and listen for his voice from within my heart. Instinctively, I knew the more I shared my life with others, the easier and more fulfilling my life would be. Together, Bodhi told me, we would all be stronger.

As I learned my lessons, I was excited to be born and could not wait to share and experience life. Little did I know, however, the many challenges awaiting me. Though life did not seem it would be difficult as I was waiting to be born, I did not understand the confusion and chaos awaiting me after I left the comfort and safety of my mother's womb.

Bodhi taught me a lot in the nine months I was waiting to be born. Among the many things I learned was the reason we are born, the meaning of life. We are born to learn and grow spiritually together, selflessly, as we are challenged every day with the many distraction's life will present us.

Bodhi is my spirit guide; he represents the intrinsic love and compassion for all living things that is a part of each of us. After I was born, however, I would discover his voice would become muted, distant, as I learned how to survive in the world. Though I would eventually remember everything he taught me while I was waiting to be born, I found it difficult to remember these things after my birth due to Anatta's, my ego's, influence on my life.

Therefore, after we are born, it is our goal to not only remember everything we were taught but also to share the knowledge and selfless love we intrinsically have with others. This understanding and inherent unconditional love is within all life; it is our higher-self. By understanding and accepting this, we can become one with our higher-self, one with god.

The primary lesson Bodhi taught me was the importance of sharing love given freely without expectations. This unconditional love is what connects all life together. Though it may often appear we are alone after we are born, we never are. We are all spiritually connected to each other. This is true of all life forms, including animals, plants, and all life on other planets in the universe as well. As I was to find out, life is not unique to our planet, but is present on many of the trillions of other planets existing within the universe as well. But I will talk of that later.

After our birth, as we learn how to survive in the world, it is common to forget what we learned while we were waiting to be born. The reason we are born, what our high-self represents, is a return to this knowledge unimpeded by the distraction's life presents us. Our spirit guide teaches us to be selfless, loving, caring, and compassionate to everyone, regardless of any perceived differences we may have. It lets us know all life is important, no one life is more important than another, and only by helping each other selflessly will the struggles we may have after we are born lessen.

As I am waiting to be born, I learn the reason we are alive is to remember what we once knew to be true when we were within our mother's womb and embrace that truth after we are exposed to the many distractions throughout our life. Our higher-self is simply a return to the spiritual path. When we can do this, the inner peace and love once existing within our mother's womb will return and permeate every fiber and cell of our body. It is a return to our spiritual-self, which was long forgotten after our birth as we learned to survive in the world.

Bodhi also tried to prepare me for what life would be like after I was born. He told me about Anatta and the many things that would distract me from remembering what he had taught me. He also told me about the two paths in life I may take: one path leading to inner peace and love and the other to confusion and fear.

As I lie here, on the last day of my life, I now remember everything he once told me. It is ironic because I did not remember anything he had told me before today, from the moment I took my first breath until now. Like so many others, I simply fell into step, doing what I was supposed to do and socialized to believe was true. The untold hardship and depression this caused me throughout my life led me to realize today my life was a failure, lived in vain. I had forgotten all the lessons Bodhi once taught me until today, the day I was to die.

I now know I am no different than the great majority of others. This lack of spiritual understanding to discover the reason we are alive is extraordinary. Many will not even consider this possibility. Others are simply too busy, confused or struggling to survive to have time to remember their spiritual origins. For those of us who follow this path, our lives will be a constant battle. Even if we are lucky enough, like I was, to be wealthy and not have to worry about money, something is still missing. Unless we understand, accept, and reengage with the spiritual part of our lives, that missing element will haunt us for the rest of our life.

Though I would be born to wealthy parents and become rich and famous while I was alive, it wasn't until today, the day I am going to die, I finally understand this. My entire life was filled with regrets, loneliness, and unhappiness. I never understood why, since I had the best life had to offer. I lived my life, as most do, following and believing what I learned after I was born, rather than everything I had learned while I waited in my mother's womb.

To discover meaning in our life, it is important to find and embrace our spiritual side and not be afraid to take a leap of faith. Being spiritual is quite different than being religious. To be spiritual is to become one with our spirit, our higher-self, accepting and following the spirit's path through life. Religion, however, is based far more on the fallacies of Anatta and what we learn in the world as we are growing up.

Though initially, religion may have had good intentions, following its ideologies will rarely lead to a spiritual awakening. Rather, it often leads to confusion, having us follow a false learned path through life. These learned emotions prevent an awakening; the love religion preaches is often conditional, based on getting something in return, rather than unconditional. Despite its early efforts to encourage sharing love in a purer manner, over the years, Anatta influenced religious interpretation to what it is today. This is true of many other positive emotions religion encourages as well and is why so many are now questioning the value religion has in their lives. Spirituality, however, only encourages unconditional love without any expectations of receiving anything in return.

Bodhi tried to prepare me for this; I thought I understood what he had taught me. In reality though, we are never really prepared or understand what to expect after we are born. The realities of trying to learn and survive in the world led me to not only forget what I originally knew to be true, but also to live a meaningless unsatisfying life.

The amazing thing about life though, is we can change the direction our life is going in. All we need is the will to do so and the knowledge of what the change needs to be. By accepting the spiritual path in life, life can change instantaneously. The veil and cloak covering our eyes and body can be lifted, revealing the path to inner peace, unconditional love, and understanding. Unlike me, it is not necessary for you to wait until the last day of your life to finally realize this; it may be done much earlier. It will take an extraordinary effort on your part to do so. I assure you though, the change will be worth it. If I had only known how to do this before today, I would have gladly made any sacrifice to achieve the inner peace and love I finally feel now. I had searched for this feeling every day of my life, never once finding it. Yet, I now know it is possible to find this much earlier in life than I did.

The Prism

When we are first born, before we are socialized and taught what to believe, the light refracted through the prism of life is pure white. This white light emerges due to the inherent wisdom and unconditional love present within each life.

As we learn how we are supposed to act and treat each other though, living in a self-centered world, the white light of the prism is dispersed into an infinite number of hues. The more we accept and believe what we are taught, the murkier the reflected colors of the rainbow flowing through the prism become. The darker the light emerging from the prism, the more challenging our life will become.

Most of humanity's self-inflicted problems and harmful emotions experienced around the world, both now and throughout history, happen when a majority see a darkened light emerging through the prism of life.

As we awaken, sensing the first loving messages from our spirit within, we begin to question the truth of what we had been taught. The colors we now see reflected through the prism begin to lighten as we start to reject much of what we once believed. The lighter the colors observed on the other side of the prism the more peaceful, loving, and meaningful our life will become.

Though we may never once again see the pure white color we knew before we were first born, it is the journey to rediscover this white light that is the genuine reason we are alive.

Chapter 4
My Birth

I was born shortly before midnight into a very noisy, cold, bright world. To be honest, it was not exactly what I expected. The warm, dark, loving womb of my mother was replaced by the chaos, cold, confusion, and noise of the world; a world I would live in for 85 years. Nothing was ever the same after I was born. With my first breath, Anatta was born as well, and she would accompany me throughout my life. Unlike Bodhi, who lived within my heart, Anatta lived in my mind and body. I did not know it at the time, but Anatta was to have a huge influence over me throughout my life. In fact, as I was to discover today, not only did Anatta dominate my life, but she did so completely. Everything I did throughout my life was dictated by her wishes. Until today, the day I am going to die, I barely heard Bodhi's voice again. His guidance, which was so pure and easy to understand before I was born, was thoroughly quieted now, hidden within my heart, awaiting my permission to reappear. I, as well as so many others, never gave him this permission. He, therefore, remained muted, waiting, hoping for me to realize he was there to help me. All I had to do to summon him was sit in a comfortable chair, close my eyes, empty my mind, listening quietly for his voice. Though I never meditated, even if I tried, I don't think I would have been able to hear him. I spent my entire life avoiding the emotional pain resulting from living in a harsh cruel world; I was simply too afraid to try.

I do not remember much about the first few years of my life. I slept a lot, but when I was awake, everything was new and exciting. My parents were very busy people who worked a lot and really did not spend much time with me. I had a nanny, Rosa, who would change my diapers, feed me, and hold me when I was crying. I was their only child, though we did have a cat and a dog as well. I liked them a lot since they would play with me. I must have been very dirty because I remember they would constantly lick me to keep me clean.

Though I did not know it, my parents were very wealthy and successful in life. There was always a lot of noise. My parents knew many people and often had big parties at our house. People would be laughing, listening to loud music, dancing, drinking alcohol, and taking drugs; they all seemed to be so happy. I knew one day, I wanted to be happy just like them.

During the first five years of my life, there was much to learn. I learned from watching my parents, their friends, my nanny, movies on the tv, and games on my children's tablet, which also allowed me to learn about the world outside my house. I saw how happy people acted and treated others; I also saw many people suffering and hurting each other in movies and shows on the tv we would watch in the evening before I went to bed. I learned this is how life is supposed to be and how we should treat each other. I saw other people not having a home to live in or food to eat. They were homeless, dressed in tattered clothes, and looked very unhappy; they often were yelled at by other people who walked by them.

In the movies, I saw violence and how easy it was to be mean and hurt other people. Many people died and, though there were some people who appeared upset about their death, it did not seem to be very important. I also learned about hunger, anger, fear, sadness, homelessness, cruelty, unhappiness, selfishness, prejudice, and worrying only about ourselves and not others. I learned all these things, and much more, were normal and what life was supposed to be like.

I also grew to know how important money was. Money not only allowed my parents to be very happy and enjoy their life, but also made them better than others. I saw how to treat other people as well by watching how my parents treated those who worked for them. They would often yell at them, telling them what to do.

During this time, I also learned how to act to get what I wanted. All I had to do was cry, yell, and demand what I wanted, and I almost always got it. Sometimes, when we left our house, I would even lie down on the floor screaming if there was something special my parents or nanny did not want to buy me; that often worked well. I was really figuring out what was important in life, and it did not seem very hard at all.

My parents and Rosa would tell me what to do and how to act. They told me I should always smile, telling others everything was great, even when I was sad, so other people would like me. Though I did not know it at the time, this was the start of a mask I was to wear for the rest of my life. This imaginary mask would completely cover my face, so my parents, Rosa, and others would like the me I projected. I knew if I smiled and acted happy, everyone would want to be around me. It did not matter how I really felt, as long as everyone else thought I was happy. I learned to wear my mask so well no one, not even Rosa or my parents, knew how I really felt about anything. In fact, I do not even think I knew how I felt either.

We lived in a big house with a swimming pool. There were three people who worked for my parents, doing everything for them; my parents were far too busy to do these things themselves. I was taken care of mostly by Rosa. As she was to tell me when I was a little older, she was born in a country far away; when she spoke, she had a funny accent I gradually grew to understand. My parents told me to let Rosa know if I needed anything; it was her job to do what I wanted and take care of me. My parents were not very nice to her; sometimes they yelled and were mean to her. Besides Rosa, there was a maid who cleaned our house and cooked our meals, as well as a gardener, who not only took care of the lawn outside but also fixed anything broken. Since my parents were wealthy and very important people, I knew they were successful and better than everyone else.

During these formative years, I did not see my parents often. Rosa did everything for me. She not only changed my diapers, but also dressed, fed, and held me if I was upset. She lived in a room in our house, so she could always come to me if I needed anything. Occasionally, my mother would hold me as well; I would get a warm feeling when she did. Most of the time, though, she was too busy. She would party a lot and, as I was to learn later, constantly drink alcohol and take drugs as well. My dad was almost never home and when he was, he would join my mother, laughing, drinking, and taking drugs, rarely spending any time with me at all.

By the time I was five years old and ready to begin school, I knew a lot about what was important in life. I also knew how to act to get others to like me. By that time, I had learned to wear my mask so well, no one really knew how I felt about anything. Though I may have been upset and sad about something, I always smiled, just like I had been taught, so no one would ever know my true feelings. Little did I know at the time, but this mask would remain with me throughout my life and rarely allowed me to experience my true emotions. Though it protected me, it also dulled my feelings. It took so much energy to keep the mask in place, but I knew how important it was not to take it off. I was grateful to my parents for teaching me how to put the mask on. After all, it helped me so much throughout my life.

I had learned my lessons well and was ready to go out and conquer the world. At five years old, I had all the answers and knew the meaning of life. The meaning of life was to only worry about myself and my happiness. I knew how to treat others, to act to get what I wanted, to hide my feelings from others, and to enjoy life by drinking alcohol and taking drugs when I was older. I knew I was better than everyone else because we were wealthy, and watching others die, be hungry, get sick, and struggle was a natural part of life. I learned all this from my parents, Rosa, movies, and from everything I saw and observed during my first five years of life. Every single time I saw how others acted and treated each other, I learned how I should act and be as well.

I must admit, this was not what I expected when I was first born, though I totally accepted this is how life was supposed to be lived. I learned I had to worry only about myself and my happiness and did not have to care about other people since I was better than them. I also realized how unimportant life was as I watched on tv people die, go hungry, not have a place to live, and be taken advantage of by others. It was often sad to watch, but eventually, before I was five years old, it did not bother me anymore. After a while, understanding these things were inevitable in the world, I even began to enjoy watching other people die and suffer, knowing those things would never happen to me.

To the Children of the World

As you are growing up, you will notice life can appear to be very challenging. The world is not always a very nice place to live in. You will see many things that make you wonder why bad things happen to so many. You will see people who do not have enough food to eat or a place to live, and others, Who do not like someone because they are different.

Regardless of what color your skin is, the country you live in, your beliefs, or any other differences there are between us, it is important you do not believe anyone is better or more important than anyone else. Every life is equally important, regardless of any differences there are between us.

Living a good life has nothing to do with the job you have, the amount of money you make, if you are famous, or anything else you may hear about when you are growing up. Rather, the only important thing is that you are a good person. Be someone who truly cares about others feelings, helping them whenever you can, treating everyone with kindness and love, even if they do not treat you that way.

You will find there are many in the world who are unhappy, afraid, and worry only about themselves. Please, do not be like them. You can change the world if you simply listen to the quiet voice in your heart and share the loving messages you hear with others. Embrace life with awe. Be kind to everyone. Share the goodness in your heart with those who are different or struggling. And, most importantly, treat others like you wish to be treated.

If you do this, you will be happy. Choose not to live in a world where everyone is afraid, worrying only about themselves. Instead, be compassionate loving, respectful, humble, and optimistic about life. Be courageous. Care about others feelings. Be friendly and help them if they are different or in need. If you do this, you may find your life will be happy and meaningful.

The path you choose through life will decide the future of the world. The older generations have not done a very good job taking care of our planet or each other. It is up to you, therefore, our children, to make the changes that must be made, by always choosing the loving path in life.

Chapter 5
School

I started school when I was five years old. It was there I was to meet a lot of other kids and learn more about the world. I already knew a lot though. I had learned much during the first five years of my life and was excited, ready to conquer the world.

I had never been around other children before; I now had to learn not only how to get along with them, but also to get them to like me. I had already learned to always smile, not show my real feelings, and had become very good at never letting anyone know how I really felt. I had mastered wearing my mask so well no one ever got to truly know me. I would obediently smile, tell everyone, including my parents, things were great. Inside, however, I did not feel that way.

I often felt anxious, stressed, and unhappy, but just as I had been taught, no one knew this. As it turned out, I was so good at doing this, I never knew my real feelings either. This was to cause me innumerable problems throughout my life; I was not able to reveal my true feelings to even those I loved, who were closest to me. I had created the perfect facade, one where everyone who met me thought I was extremely happy. Though inside, I felt depressed, alone, and completely miserable.

I remember one day, at one of the many parties my parents had in our house, I woke up scared and afraid. I went downstairs to find my mother, wanting her to tell me everything would be alright. Not only was I scared and afraid, but I had been feeling sad for a long time as well. When I finally found my mother with her friends, I obediently smiled as I had been taught. I told my mother I had woken up and was scared; she hugged me, telling me everything would be alright. Though I felt better, the one thing I most remember from that occasion, was how proud my mother was when her friends told her what a nice, happy girl I was. Though I felt afraid and sad, nobody knew it, not even my parents, their friends, or Rosa. I knew then I had succeeded in life and would never let anyone know my true feelings again. After all, I wanted my parents to love me. The sadness I felt was severe depression, which continued throughout my life. It was not until several years later though, when I was a teenager, my parents finally realized something was wrong and sent me to a doctor and counselor to get help.

When I was seven years old, I did something at school that got me into trouble. I hit another little girl when she did not do what I wanted her to. Everyone was mad at me, telling me what I did was wrong. I began to cry and felt hurt. I was embarrassed as the other kids were laughing at the sight of me in trouble and upset. I remember this day so well because, at that very moment, my heart hardened as Anatta put up a wall to protect me. This wall surrounded my heart and would never let me be hurt or embarrassed again.

I did not know it at the time, but the wall did much more than protect me. It also surrounded Bodhi, imprisoning him within my heart as well. On the day I was going to die, my wall finally shattered, allowing Bodhi to clearly talk with me once more. Though Bodhi told me he had always been with me, the wall Anatta created to protect me when I was seven years old had kept his voice muted. As I listened to him now, I was incredibly sad, realizing what I had missed by not involving him more in my life.

Before I tell you about the rest of my childhood, I really need to tell you more about the wall, which affected my life every single day since Anatta built it when I was a child. I really liked the wall; it protected me from many bad things that were to happen to me throughout the rest of my life. In my mind, it was made of steel and was impenetrable. No one could ever hurt or embarrass me again; with the wall intact, I could no longer feel emotional pain. From that moment until today, the day I am going to die, I never cried. What I did not know, however, is that the wall also prevented me from hearing Bodhi's voice again.

Instead, all the emotions I felt, from that day forward, were taught to me by Anatta. I learned love was conditional; I only gave it if it benefited me. I also grew to understand everything I learned during the first five years of my life was true; life was hard. I had to worry about myself first and not others. Anatta taught me about many other emotions as well. Besides conditional love, she taught me about hate, fear, worry, sadness, prejudice, and much more. I also understood what was important in life; it was me.

I spent the rest of my life believing this. Unfortunately, I think the great majority of people believe this as well. I lived my entire life in fear of everything. And with fear, came many other negative emotions and feelings. I was severely depressed, though I never truly understood why. I also was afraid of being hurt, both physically and emotionally, though my wall protected me from the latter. I was grateful for the wall and mask because they kept me from feeling the pain we suffer every day, living in a chaotic, often cruel world.

As I was to learn today, on the last day of my life, by living my life in fear, rather than with love, I had surrendered to the inevitability and negativity of life. I saw life as hard, embracing all the negative emotions and actions I learned when I was growing up. Seeing the world through this lens skewed my true understanding about how I viewed the world. I viewed life as competitive; I, therefore, knew my only concern was for myself and my happiness. I never considered there may be another way to see life. I fully accepted this view of the world; this was how it was supposed to be. The idea of sharing my love unselfishly was foreign to me, as my wall prevented Bodhi from talking to me again until today.

The Mask and the Wall

We learn, often when we are young children, how to conceal our true emotions behind a mask we may wear and a wall we build, becoming very adept at hiding almost all our feelings from others and, often, even from ourselves.

The mask and wall help us survive in a self-centered world, allowing our responses to different situations to be socially acceptable. It is not easy though to continually wear a mask or hide behind a wall. The larger the mask and the more of our face it covers, the thicker the wall surrounding our heart, the greater the problems we will have in our life and the more stress and anxiety we may experience and feel.

We must all strive to rip off the mask and tear down the wall preventing us from reaching our full potential. If we do, allowing our spirit to become the primary guide in our life, We will be finally be able to experience life as it was truly meant to be.

Chapter 6
My Life as a Teenager

T

he next seven years of my life went by quickly. I almost never heard Bodhi anymore; he was trapped behind the wall within my heart. Instead, I continued to learn from Anatta as she taught me everything I needed to know to be happy in the world. Everyone and everything was my teacher. I would learn from watching my parents, their friends, other kids at school, movies, and the internet. I saw so much violence on tv and my video games, I eventually became immune, numb watching other people suffering and dying.

From my parents, I learned drinking and taking drugs led to having a good time and, since they were wealthy, they did not have to treat other people with respect. I understood they were better than everyone else since they were successful. I would watch their friends at the many parties they had at our house. Everyone was laughing, dancing, drinking, taking drugs, making out, and having fun; I knew I wanted to have fun just like they did.

From other kids in school, since I dressed better than they did and came from a good family, I discovered I was better than they were. Just as my parents treated Rosa and the other people who worked for them as inferior, I knew I could treat other kids who were not as good as me the same way. I did have some friends, though they looked like me and came from families who were successful as well.

I knew the only way to survive in the world was to worry about and take care of myself. My parents often told me we lived in a harsh, competitive world and I needed to worry only about myself and not others. It did not bother me anymore when I read about people who died because of war, murder, starvation, illness, or other reasons. Eventually, I learned to mostly ignore this.

When I was twelve years old, I began hanging out with other kids who liked to party and have a good time, just like my parents. We would listen to music, dance, and drink alcohol we stole from our parents' homes. Since a lot of us had parents who were wealthy, we would also steal money from them and buy drugs to help us feel better, having learned from our parents, watching movies, and reading stories, we knew this is how to enjoy life.

Life was great; I could now understand why these things made you so happy. I was living in a constant daze; my mind was clouded as I went through life enjoying the high the drugs and alcohol gave me. By this time, I almost never heard from Bodhi anymore. He was a very distant memory; I assumed he simply left me. Therefore, I only listened to and followed everything Anatta told me. Soon after I turned 14 years old, I began to have sex and really enjoyed it. I then realized how much power I had over the boys I slept with; they would do anything for me if I took care of them.

Not a day passed I did not drink or take drugs. I often started early, before I went to school and would continue when I would get together with my friends after school. I was living life to the fullest now, just like my parents did. I really do not remember much of my early teenage years; the memories are clouded by all the drugs, alcohol, and sex. I just remember I had a good time, was high most of the time, partied every day, and had sex with many different boys. Life was wonderful.

As I got older, when I was 16 years old, I auditioned to be in a movie about a girl who partied every day, took drugs, drank alcohol, and had a lot of sex. To be honest, this was my life, so it was a role I was intimately familiar with. I got the part and the movie was a huge success; after that, I became very famous and went on to make many other movies. I was also beautiful, now standing at 5 foot 8 inches, weighing only 125 pounds. With dark hair and blue eyes, I was also well endowed, which allowed me to get almost anything I wanted from men for the rest of my life. With my success making movies, I became very wealthy on my own as well. Since I understood how important money was to make me happy, I knew my life was going to be very successful.

I continued to party, drink alcohol, and take drugs every day. I am not sure how I did it, but it did not affect my acting career. I always remembered my lines; and because of the mask I wore, I was easily able to communicate any emotion I wanted. Acting was so easy for me; after all, I had been acting my entire life. The lifelong play I was in required me to be happy, smile and ignore pain, and I had mastered this role long ago.

I had learned my lessons well and was grateful to my parents for teaching me how to survive in the world. Though my severe depression continued afflicting me throughout my life, the mask I wore and the wall I erected protected me and allowed me to be someone else. In fact, I was so good at hiding my real feelings I won several prestigious awards throughout my career for the range of emotions I was able to project.

What I had not known, however, until today, was my depression, sadness and struggles through life were caused by the mask and wall I had put up to protect me. By shielding me, they also isolated my authentic higher-self and by doing this, allowed the feelings and emotions I learned in the world to dominate my life. As I was to find out today, on the last day of my life, the anxiety, depression, sadness and other emotions and feelings I felt were a result of Bodhi calling out to me, trying to get my attention, to let me know I was following the wrong path through life. He was attempting to tell me the self-centered path I had chosen was causing all my problems. By making me uncomfortable, anxious, and depressed, he hoped I would reexamine my life and choose a different path, though I never did.

Such times in our life, when we are stressed and feel a tight knot in our stomach, afflict everyone. We know something is wrong, though have no idea what it may be. Perhaps the next time this happens to you, consider the possibility this feeling is caused by your Spirit guide trying to get your attention as well.

The Play

On the day we are going to die, when the ego, our self-centered beliefs, finally surrenders its hold on our life, we will understand our entire life was a play; it was all make-believe. We acted our part so well we never knew it was not real.

Life is just an illusion, where we all have our bit parts in the play. If we follow the script, as we learned to do as we are growing up, the answers we seek about life may elude us. It is only when we act outside the boundaries of the script and awaken, the answers we seek may finally begin to reveal themselves.

Chapter 7
My Life as an Adult

A

fter I finished high school, I did not need to go to college. By this time, I had already acted in three movies and was becoming a very good actress. All the experiences I had since I was little, wearing a mask over my face to disguise my real feelings from others, helped me easily become someone else. I could laugh or cry on demand, as I had done many times growing up, to get what I wanted. It did not even feel like I had to try hard; I was very good at hiding my real feelings. I had long ago learned how to act, masking my true feelings from everyone around me.

Since I was considered gorgeous by all men, I never lacked for company. I eventually got married four times and had three children as well. Like my parents, I too was very busy; too busy to spend much time with my children. And like my parents, I had a full-time nanny to take care of them and a housekeeper to cook and clean since I was working away from home most of the time.

My housekeeper's name was Cherish. Cherish was a big, dark skinned woman whose family came from Africa. She had four children at home and had to take three different buses to get to our house. It took her over an hour to get to our upscale neighborhood from her home, yet she never once complained. We paid her what I thought was a fair wage of $10/hr.

Cherish was always smiling and happy. She would sing native African songs while she worked and always had a good word to say to everyone in my family. The kids absolutely adored Cherish. She would spend hours with them after school telling them stories of Africa. When they were small, she would sit in the rocking chair, put them on her lap and sing African children's songs she had learned when she was young.

Over the next few years, I got to know Cherish well. She told me life in Africa, where she grew up, was very hard. There was always a shortage of food, her clothes were old and tattered and her family, which consisted of her mother, father, four brothers and sisters, and her grandfather, all lived in a small one-room home with a thatched roof that often leaked when it rained. They also had no running water or a bathroom.

Despite all this, Cherish had nothing but wonderful memories growing up. She came to the United States when she was 19 years old, got married, and quickly had four children. Her husband worked full time at a minimum wage job, so they did not have much money. They rented a small 2-bedroom apartment, where all six of them lived, and the rent alone took up almost half of what her husband made.

But there was something strange about Cherish. She was happy, truly happy. She often talked fondly of her husband and children and there was almost an aura emanating around her I can only describe as a glow. She never once felt sorry for herself, either for how she grew up or her life now. Though she had very little money, she was at peace and happy. The way she talked about her family, it was obvious they had unconditional love for each other. She felt that same love for her family and friends in Africa.

How could someone who did not have all the things I had, be so happy and have so much love? I knew having many material things was necessary to being happy. Yet, despite her upbringing in the Congo, her living conditions here, and having so little money for her family of six, she was full of joy and love for everyone. Could it be possible you could be poor, a different race, not famous or beautiful, and still be happy and know love? For many years, I could not appreciate how this could be. It was not until the last day of my life I finally understood.

Instead, I would begin drinking and using cocaine when I first got up in the morning, continuing throughout the day until I went to sleep. I liked the dazed feeling I had, numbing the feelings of severe depression and sadness I was to have throughout my life. If I kept busy, dulling my feelings with work, alcohol, drugs, and sex, I did not have to think about or confront the cause of my depression and unhappiness directly. I, therefore, chose to live my life, as my parents had done, staying busy and partying. When I was not busy, my depression became worse, often to the point I felt suicidal. So, I rarely let that happen.

During this time, I bought a big house with a pool, had several sports cars and the best material possessions money could buy. I knew all these things would make me happy. I traveled a lot around the world, not only for work, but for fun as well. I was seldom alone, as I knew many people and had quite a few friends as well. Life was very good to me.

The many movies I made often took me to exotic locations around the world. There, I met many people, partying every night, drinking lots of alcohol and taking drugs daily. I rarely slept alone and almost never with the same person twice. What everyone saw was a very happy, sexy, wealthy, fun-loving woman who was always smiling; I was always the life of the party. The mask I wore was so successful at hiding the pain and depression I constantly lived with, no one ever knew how I really felt; in fact, I did not even know my true feelings either. Since I was famous and wealthy, I had a very successful life.

I could not understand why I felt so depressed, alone, and unhappy. No one knew, but behind the façade I projected to the world, I was miserable. It did not make sense to me. How could I feel alone, yet always be surrounded by other people? And how could I be depressed and unhappy when I was wealthy and had so much?

There were countless days I wanted to end the unrelenting pain I felt within. I had thought of killing myself many times, though something within me kept me from doing so. As I found out much later, on the last day of my life, this something was Bodhi. Somehow, he was able to give me just enough hope, even though he was locked behind an impenetrable wall within my heart. Those who are unable to tolerate the pain they experience within and choose to end their lives are often unable to hear their spirit guide during those last moments. Unfortunately, there are many people who choose this path.

If you have ever wondered how someone rich, famous, and beautiful, who appears to have everything can commit suicide, you now have your answer. It is because our lives lack meaning, causing us to become severely depressed and unhappy. We looked for meaning in the world or through being with another person and, not finding it there, we are confused. Everything we had learned told us we should be happy, yet we are not.

As I was to find out, just before I was ready to die, we were unhappy because we were seeking love and happiness in the wrong place. The answers to life, love, and happiness, may only be found within our heart, where our spirit exists, and may not be found elsewhere. Only by sharing our love selflessly, not just with those closest to us, but with everyone else as well, will we find what we have always searched for. The many barriers Anatta erects, including the mask and wall, and all we have learned and accepted to be true throughout our lives confuses us, leading us to follow a false path through life.

As I traveled around the world, I saw extreme poverty and the struggles many people face throughout their lives. I saw children dying of starvation and illnesses we had cures for; they were too poor to be able to afford food or the medications needed to treat their illness. Many of these poor people and children, though, appeared happy. I could not understand how they could feel joy, not having money or leading a successful life. Their lives were a failure; I was just glad my life was not. I was rich, famous, and sexy, and therefore, I knew I was leading a very successful life.

One of the movies I made was in Africa. Seeing how poor many people in Africa were, the hunger, sickness, fear of death from war, and the many other struggles they faced every day, made me grateful for everything I had. On the movie set, we lived in luxury compared to everyone else. I had learned, when I was a child, there was nothing I could do to change anything or make others' lives better, so, as everyone around me, I too ignored everything I saw.

The story I am about to tell you though is about one little girl I met while I was making this movie in Africa. Her name was Salama, which is an African name that means peace. Salama was ten years old, happy, and always had a smile on her face; she also spoke English quite well. Salama, like many other children from a nearby village, was very curious about the movie we were making and often came to watch as we filmed every day. She was fascinated with everything, and one day, between scenes, I met her as I was walking back to my trailer to rest.

What struck me most was her smile and the aura radiating around her for all to see. Not only did she seem happy, but she appeared to be at peace as well; something I had never felt throughout my life. I was curious how someone so young and poor could be happy and at peace; she did not appear to have anything. She wore a ragged old dress and sandals on her feet, which were falling apart.

As we were making the movie over the next few months, we got to know each other better. We talked a lot and Salama told me about herself, her family, and her life in the nearby village where she lived. Salama lived with her father, mother, grandfather, two sisters and a brother in a small hut that was just big enough for them to lie down at night to sleep. Her parents worked hard trying to make enough money to buy food to eat and clothes to wear to protect them from the elements. It was clear Salama loved her family very much.

One day, her family invited me to dinner. Since we were taking a small break from the movie, I gladly accepted their invitation. When we got to her village, the first thing that struck me was how happy all the people in the village were to meet me. They were all smiling and laughing, coming up and welcoming me. The village itself was small and had about twenty huts in it; the huts were small and some of them appeared to need repair.

Salama's family was wonderful. They greeted me with joy, hugging me as I entered their hut. I remember wondering how seven people could live in such a small hut, but they appeared not to be concerned at all. Dinner consisted of traditional African foods. One of these foods was called chakalaka, which is a vegetable dish made of onions, tomatoes, peppers, carrots, beans, and spices, which they grew themselves in their small garden. We also had pap, a kind of porridge, which is a starchy dish made from white corn maize, similar to grits I had eaten in the south. The food was delicious, and I was grateful for the opportunity to get to know a traditional African family and eat a traditional meal with them.

Though Salama's grandfather did not speak English, the rest of her family did. What I remember most from this dinner was how happy and gracious they all were. Though they had little food or possessions, it did not appear to matter to them. They did not understand they were not successful in life because they did not have a lot of money or own many nice things. Their joy appeared real and came from their heart. It did not make sense to me; I knew success only came from money and having the best things in life.

As I would find out from Bodhi, on the last day of my life, Salama's family was happy because they did not have walls or masks to hide their true self. They were authentic; they had never learned success in life was determined by looks, wealth, and possessions. Instead, they defined success a different way. To them, success was being together, having enough food to eat, clothes to wear, shelter from the elements, and sharing their love of life selflessly with each other. They understood this was the meaning of life.

Since Anatta did not teach them any of the other things in the world defining success, they simply did not know about them. Their lives, though simple, were truly happy, for they defined success as coming from within their heart, rather than coming from what they could buy or find in the world. Through their simplicity, they knew what many of us struggle to discover every day. They knew happiness and meaning do not come from all the things we think they come from in the world; rather they come from within, from the unconditional love we share with each other.

I also saw many different types of wild animals during those months in Africa. Whenever I was able to get a glimpse into their eyes, I would sense a spirit within them as well; it was then I realized animals have a spirit as well. If you have ever had a pet, perhaps a cat or dog, then you know how true this is. That must give us all pause to think.

I wondered if the animals I saw had feelings and sought love as we do. I believed they did, especially if you see the bond between a mother and her babies. I saw mothers surrender their lives to predators just to save their babies and allow them to escape. Think how many spirit guides there must be if each animal also has one. And if we further believe that plants, since they also have life, have spirit guides, then this number would be astronomical. We all, whether human or animal, appear to seek the same two things: love and companionship. I came to understand this as I observed the herds of animals traveling and living together and the many extended families in the animal kingdom. It made me realize we are all not that different after all.

What I also knew to be true, despite my wall and mask, was I found working a lot to be very therapeutic. There are many others who are workaholics. We work a lot not only to survive and make money, but also so we do not have time left to confront our past or unhappiness. Just like me, if you do not have any free time, you will not have to confront your demons either. We convince ourselves we must work hard to be successful; of course, it really depends on what your definition of success is. If success to you is the same as it was for me, I assure you, you will never find it regardless of how much money you make or material possessions you own.

If, however, you learn what Salama and her family already knew, success has little to do with money but rather with something else, then you may feel different. Success to them was being able to be their authentic-self, one unsullied by the many distractions' life presents every day. Though I was successful, as defined by society and all I had learned throughout my life, in reality, Salama and her family, having very little money or possessions, were far more successful than I was. For them, success was defined by a different criteria: the actual love and respect they had for themselves, each other, and all life. They, therefore, understood the true meaning of life far better than I was ever to.

There was another movie I made early in my acting career that made me question everything I was taught as well. This movie was made in the United States, among one of the Native American tribes still living on the reservation they were consigned to. It was the second movie I ever made; I was seventeen years old. The role I played was that of a teenage girl whose parents were killed; I was kidnapped and taken to live with the Lakota Nation in North Dakota. At first, I was treated very badly, especially by the Native American women. Eventually, though, after I had been there for some years, I met and married a warrior and was gradually accepted as one of their own.

The reason I am telling this story is because there is much we can all learn from the beliefs of these proud people. The Lakota believed animals, plants, and humans all came from one source: Mother Earth. Animals were respected as equals to humans. Of course, they were hunted, but only for food, and the hunter always first asked permission of the animal's spirit. They also believed each creature, including humans, had its own spirit or Wakan, and this spirit came from one universal source: the Great Spirit or Wakan Tanka. As I can now finally appreciate, on the last day of my life, there is so much we can all learn from following many of the Lakota beliefs and traditions. Rather than learn from them though, we committed genocide on not only the Lakota, but all other Native American tribes as well.

As I was making movies, the wall Anatta built when I was seven years old had become thicker and stronger. No light was able to penetrate the wall; it was solid. As Bodhi was later to tell me, on the last day of my life, I could not hear him because he was trapped behind the wall. There was only quiet and darkness within; the only voice I could hear was Anatta. The mask Anatta created to hide my true feelings from others remained intact as well. Though I thought I knew what love was, I did not. I thought love was what I observed in the movies, romantic love, and though it may have lasted for a while, in my case four times, the love eventually ended.

For many who retire from work, they suddenly have free time and are forced to think. They begin to question many of their choices as they finally have time to confront the demons they avoided for years by staying so busy. Now having time to review their lives, they often become depressed and anxious, as they must examine their own mask and wall they too erected as a child to protect them from the chaos and pain of living in the world. Most, like me, will also not be able break through these obstacles until the last day of their lives. Only then may they begin to understand, as I did, the many poor choices they made throughout their life as well.

It is sad to realize how many of us do not find our answers until the very end of our life; we had to endure so much pain, anxiety, and depression every day. The hardest thing about knowing this is that it all was unnecessary. Our lives passed us by, engulfing us in loneliness and pain, simply because we followed the false path of Anatta, rather than the true path of our spirit. How many of us wonder, in those last days, what it would be like to have a do-over, be able to go back to our childhood understanding what we know today. Imagine living life without a mask or a wall, knowing where to find the answers we seek earlier in our life, realizing all we had to do to awaken, become Enlightened and find inner peace and happiness, was to sit in a comfortable chair, close our eyes, quiet our mind, and listen. Instead, most of us struggle all our lives, seeking our answers in the world or from being with another person, where true happiness may never be found. The irony of life is we spend our entire lives trying to return to the knowledge we once had before we were born, before we were exposed to everything we were to learn from others after we left the comfort of our mother's womb.

Think about how our words and actions can affect the lives of every person we interact with. My wall was erected from a single incident when I was seven years old; it was to have a profound effect on me for the rest of my life. Imagine what life could be like if we treated each other, all life forms, and the earth, with the respect and care we all desire for ourselves. Instead of competition, there would be cooperation, and instead of living our lives with hate and fear, we would live our lives with love and compassion.

Imagine.

Ubuntu – The Divine Spark of Kindness

'I am because we are.' Ubuntu is an African philosophy meaning love, truth, peace, happiness, and all other positive inherent traits present within each life. It is the essence, the divine spark of kindness, present within every life, shared without motive, for the benefit of all.

This is the world we are meant to live in; a world of unconditional love, shared selflessly with all, rather than a world of endless darkness, concerned only for ourselves.

Chapter 8
My life at 60

W

hen I was filming movies around the world, everything I learned as I was growing up was reaffirmed. It does not matter what country or continent I was working in, the many problems our species has caused each other, other life forms and to the environment, are evident everywhere.

In Africa, I saw hunger so extreme, the ribs of little children were almost popping out of their skin. Many of these children end up dying, so emaciated and weak from starvation, they could barely move or open their eyes before their life ended. I also saw many, both children and adults, dying from treatable illnesses like AIDS, tuberculosis, and malaria.

War also appeared to be going on in almost every continent I visited. Rebel groups would indiscriminately drive into different villages, killing everyone due to greed or simply because they did not believe as they did. It did not matter to them if there were women or little children in the village either; they killed them as well.

When I was making a movie in Thailand, in neighboring Cambodia, millions were killed when their leader, Pol Pot, decided to relocate his population to labor camps in the countryside. There were mass executions, forced labor, physical abuse, malnutrition, and disease that caused almost twenty five percent of the population of that country to die.

In Central America, gangs and revolutionaries wandered throughout many countries, killing at will. To be honest, I really do not know why they were doing this; it may have been for a political reason, though I think it really was due to greed, fear, and hate.

In Mexico, which I went to many times to not only work, but also on vacation, there were drug cartels so violent they not only killed many policemen but also would kill many innocent people and each other as well. Over 150,000 people were murdered over a period of seven years because of these drug cartels.

In Beijing, China, the pollution was so bad the thick air made breathing difficult, causing everyone to wear a mask when they walked outside. The severe pollution, contributing to worsening climate change, if left unchecked, will change the world as we know it today, within the next few generations.

I read about many other atrocities and genocides as well, too many to mention here, occurring both today and throughout history. From the Native Americans who were slaughtered by the Europeans, to the Aborigines whose population decreased from 1.5 million when the British first came to Australia in 1788 to less than 100,000 by the early 1900s. This list, unfortunately, could go on indefinitely; I believe you understand my point though. These deaths were unnecessary, a result of greed, hate, prejudice, and fear, which are emotions we learn after we are born into this tragic world. It would not be, until today, the day I was going to die, I would finally understand the real reasons for this, but I will discuss that later in my story.

By the time I was sixty years old, I had done everything you could do to be happy. I had traveled all over the world, was very wealthy, had three children, and three (soon to be four) ex-husbands. I also had many friends I partied with as well. I was busy almost every moment of every day, yet I was still depressed and unhappy, despite having everything anyone could want. Though I knew many people, had a family and children, I somehow felt I was all alone; no one was close to me. All my relationships and friendships were superficial thanks to the mask and the wall that had protected me throughout my life.

My three children were mostly raised by their nanny, like I was, and did not want to have anything to do with me. We were estranged and rarely talked or saw each other. The love I had showed them when they were growing up was superficial, since it was taught to me by Anatta rather than Bodhi.

They are so busy now with their own lives and children, they have little time for me. They rarely called, and when they did, they told me everything is fine. They were just like me; they learned very early in their lives to mask their real feelings as well. As I did, they too had a façade fooling everyone. I knew I must have been a good parent because they learned how to do this as well as I had.

All the people I knew were only with me because I was famous, wealthy, beautiful, and liked to have a good time. I still drank alcohol and took drugs every day to help me cope, but the drugs and alcohol no longer helped me feel better. Even though I knew many people, I felt alone and was very lonely. There were many days now, I felt my life was not worth living anymore; I wanted to kill myself, so I would not have to feel the emotional pain I had felt my entire life anymore. I was still taking medications and seeing a counselor every week for my depression, but nothing seemed to make me feel better. I could not understand, since I had lived a good life, had the best of everything, and was successful, why I felt this way. Despite having three children and eight grandchildren, they resented me for my inability to love them while they were growing up and wanted little to do with me now.

One day, as I sat alone by my pool, I started to remember when I was a child. I remembered being a toddler and told I should smile, tell everyone I was great, and not let anyone know how I was really feeling. I wanted to be liked and knew this would make my parents and Rosa happy.

I remembered putting on the mask, which was to cover my face for the rest of my life. I also remembered being seven years old, crying and being embarrassed at school, and Anatta deciding to help me by erecting a very thick wall around my heart. I remembered thanking her for doing this; I never wanted to feel that way again and I never did.

At the edge of the water, I began to realize I had never discarded the mask or been able to break through the wall Anatta imprisoned Bodhi behind. As for the wall, it was so thick, no light could penetrate it, and nothing would ever be able to hurt me again. It protected me my entire life, but at the same time, today I finally began to understand, it kept me from allowing anyone to get close to me or know how I truly felt as well.

Now, being sixty years old, I began remembering all the things I learned that were to affect my beliefs and actions for the rest of my life. Though I had lived my life to the fullest and tried to enjoy every minute by emulating what my parents had done, I sat there miserable, unhappy, alone, and severely depressed.

I thought about the many movies I had made and the people I met as I traveled throughout the world. I remembered Salama in Africa and how sincerely happy she and her family were even though they were so poor and had few material possessions. I met many others as well throughout the years who also appeared to be happy and at peace, even though they too struggled every day just to have a place to live or buy enough food for their family so they would not be hungry. I began to wonder how they could feel this way, since their lives were not successful.

I began to question everything I had thought and believed to be true, though I simply could not make sense of any of it. I lived my life, as I had always done, seeking my answers and happiness from everything I did and bought. My life, since I was little, was destined to follow this path, ever since I surrendered my happiness to Anatta and discarded what Bodhi had taught me.

Who I was, my authentic emotions and feelings, remained locked away in my heart, prevented from being revealed by the wall protecting me since I was seven years old. All the emotions I was able to show were learned, rather than sincerely felt, as they would have been, if I could have exposed my frailties and vulnerabilities. There is a big difference between learned and inherent emotions. Learned emotions (or pseudo emotions) come from our interactions in the world; we act as we think we are supposed to by observing others who showed us what these emotions are. Inherent emotions, however, come from deep within where our spirit is. These emotions are heartfelt and given freely with compassion and love.

Despite knowing something was not right, the next twenty-five years of my life went by quickly. As I became older, I continued to act in movies and had many admirers. I even got married again; though, like all my other marriages, it too did not last very long. Since I still was not able to open up and reveal my true emotions and feelings, I treated my last husband as I did the first three, looking only for what was best for me and my happiness.

After a few years, living with him became tedious and we ended up going our separate ways. Although I knew the first three marriages ended because of how my husbands had acted, this time, I wondered if perhaps I may have had something to do with our separation as well. I also wondered if my depression and loneliness may have something to do with how I treated others, rather than because no one else was as good as I was.

I began questioning things I had taken for granted since I was a child. I continued to take several medications for my depression, saw a counselor, and partied often, but nothing changed or improved. As I was to find out, on the last day of my life, it was because I still was unable to hear the messages from Bodhi. The medications and counselors were treating the physical and emotional problems I was having, but they did not treat the real underlying problem, which was spiritual. My problems were the result of not being able to hear or live the life my spirit guide wanted me to. So, these interventions proved to be only temporary and inadequate.

I did not realize or know any of this until just before my death, though I truly wish I had. Perhaps, my life could have been different if I understood this before now. But today, as I prepare to die, I know it is too late for me, but it may not be too late for you.

Our Choice in Life: I or We

There are but two paths we may pursue in life. One is the path of 'I', the ego. We learn about 'I' as we are being raised to accept society's rules and self-centered philosophy about life, always considering what is best for ourself, before we think about the effect it may have on others.

The other path we may choose is the path of 'we', the spirit. Those who follow this path always consider others in all their decisions, doing what is best for everyone. Those who follow the path of 'I', regardless of their success or accomplishments in life, will lead a life of mediocrity. Those who follow the path of 'we', however, will discover authentic love, inner peace, and the genuine meaning of life.

Which path we choose is a choice we each make; we may change the direction of our life anytime. All it takes is a willingness to listen to the quiet voice within, embrace its wisdom and unconditional loving messages, then selflessly share them with all others.

Chapter 9
Today I Am Going to Die

Part 1

I never knew how different life could have been if I had followed Bodhi's spiritual path. It appeared to me, almost from my first breath, everything in my life was never the same. As I lie here waiting to die, I feel despondent as I review my life. Though I had a very successful life, by society's standards, the reality could not be further from the truth.

I did everything right, just as I had been taught, yet, as my life flashes before me today, I realized not only was I alone, but also, I was depressed my entire life. I used drugs and alcohol, just like my parents had done, to mask my unhappiness and dull my senses. Now, I finally understood the drugs and alcohol kept me from facing the reality of how I really felt. They were a distraction preventing me from looking at myself, facing what my life was really like.

I was so successful not facing my pain it took until today, the day I am going to die, to realize my life had been lived in vain. I am alone today; no one, not even my family, is here to say goodbye or will miss me. After I die, I will be buried, though the many beautiful expensive things I had acquired during my life will not accompany me. Instead, my body will be put in a coffin or urn, just like everyone else, and I will not be able to take anything with me. All the money I have will be worthless, as it will not accompany me either.

Though I know many people will go to my funeral, all of them will have been acquaintances, people who will miss me because I was famous, not be because I was a good person or lived a worthwhile life. I am not even sure my three children will be there.

I suddenly wish I did not have to spend my last day reviewing my life because what I saw, as my life slowly flashed before me, was not pleasant. Everything I did during my life was for me, to assure I enjoyed my life to the fullest. I now know, through the clarity of Bodhi's eyes, my life was a dismal failure. On this last day of my life, Anatta finally released her hold on me, as she does on everyone when death is near. Anatta no longer has a vested interest in controlling our actions on this day. For when our body perishes, she will die as well.

I now clearly see I lived an insignificant life, one without consequence or meaning. I finally even know why I was depressed my entire life. It was because I was blindly following the path I learned from Anatta, as I was growing up and my entire life, rather than the path I was supposed to follow, the path Bodhi had told me about before I was born. From the moment of my birth, I forgot everything Bodhi had taught me as I waited to be born in my mother's womb. He had told me I would forget, but, of course, I did not remember that either.

It is only today I finally understand what that purpose is. I wish someone could have found this sooner, so I could have time to make amends and changes in my life before it was too late. Though all the doctors and counselors I saw were well-meaning, they simply were not treating me correctly. By ignoring the root of my problem, the internal conflict between Bodhi and Anatta, they were all destined to fail. If only these well-meaning people could have opened their minds and hearts, perhaps things may have been different.

I feel sorry for all those who are depressed as I was trying to get help. Due to the spiritual ignorance of many in the psychiatric and medical community, they too may never fully recover from their depression or illness. Unless the underlying spiritual cause is treated as well, not only their symptoms, I fear little will change to truly help them.

Another crushing truth I have just realized is I now know what a successful life really is. Ironically, it is almost the exact opposite of what I believed it to be. Success in life is freeing your spirit and leading a selfless life, rather than a selfish life only focused on your own enjoyment. Freeing our authentic self, our higher-self, from behind the wall of imprisonment will give our lives new purpose, one not only helping treat our depression, but also leading to a feeling of inner peace and giving meaning to our lives as well.

As I lie here, waiting to die, I now know the meaning of life is to return to the knowledge we once had before we were born; the pure authentic selfless love once radiating from within before we were exposed to the realities and teachings of the world. Before Anatta was born, before I took my first breath, I knew about inner peace and unconditional love. After I was born, however, for the next 85 years, I simply forgot.

I understood, as we all did, within my mother's womb, sharing, empathy, compassion, and unconditional love were the qualities that would make a life successful. These qualities are inherent, not learned (pseudo emotions). The emotions I am talking about are given without expectation of receiving anything in return, becoming a part of our DNA; it is what we must strive to remember and return to after we are born.

Pseudo emotions are learned emotions. After we are born, we learn about these emotions by watching movies, observing people, and simply by living life. I never understood any of this until today. I only knew how to express learned emotions during my life; those emotions I was exposed to after I was born. I, as many others are, was too afraid to ever reveal the inherent loving emotions we all possess and are born with, which allow us to get close to others.

I am writing this book to share what I have learned today. I think it is important for you, the reader, to assess which emotions you are willing to share with others as well. Pseudo emotions will only lead to loneliness and unhappiness; it is only when you share the inherent emotions we are all born with, life's meaning becomes evident.

I know now why we are alive, the meaning of life. I spent my entire life searching for this simple answer and never found it. I write this book today with the hope you may find this answer sooner than I and have more time than I did while you are alive to enjoy life as it was meant to be lived.

What is Important in Life?

The time we have left as we approach death is an interesting time in life. Many things, once thought to be important, no longer are. We begin to realize life really is not that complicated or complex; rather, it is quite simple.

The money, material possessions, job we had, and almost everything else we once thought defined what a successful life is, no longer matter. Nothing will accompany us when we die. We finally realize none of those things are, or ever were important.

Do not wait until the end of your life to decide what is truly important. To discover what is important, close your eyes, silence your mind, and listen to the quiet messages in between your racing thoughts.

Part 2

O
n this day, as I wait for my life to end, I am given a gift by Bodhi. Without Anatta's influence, he reveals to me what my life could have been if only I had been able to know what I do today. I am given a view of what leading a selfless life would be, one in which I could clearly hear my spirit guide and become one with my higher-self.

It is a life I could not even imagine before today. My life, as are many lives, was dominated by fear rather than love. I was afraid of everything and, rather than confront that fear, I simply acknowledged living in fear was normal. I accepted the reality life was meant to be difficult. Everything from war, murder, hate, homelessness, illness, and hunger proved me right about how hard life was. I accepted not only these realities, but also became immune to the effects they should have had on me. Instead, I blindly accepted these atrocities as an inevitable part of life.

Today, things are different though. What is it I can see today? I see a world where there is love, empathy, and compassion for everyone; a world where selflessness is the dominate trait, rather than only concern for ourselves. I now know what our higher-self is; it is sharing and helping each other as we all navigate through the many difficulties life presents us. Success is defined by everyone succeeding, as we help each other through life's many challenges.

On a personal level, I feel an inner peace I never knew was possible for the first time in my life. The depression and sadness that were always present no longer haunt me, being replaced instead by hope and happiness. In my mind, I can see a clear blue sky and colorful planet, whose vibrant colors are pure and pristine. There are no clouds covering the sky or pollution destroying the planet; there is just the crystal-clear colors of life offering no impedance to its beauty and purity.

It is only now, on my last day, I finally understand why I was born and the purpose of life. Though I feel inner peace, I also understand I had traveled the wrong path through life. I saw how self-destructive I had been and how selfish I was. All my relationships, including with my family, were superficial. I allowed no one to get close to me, including my husbands or children. Instead, I went through life alone, isolating my real feelings from everyone else. I had lived my life looking for happiness and meaning in the world. I was rich, had a very prestigious job as an actress, and was able to buy and do all the best things life had to offer. Yet, I know now, my life was insignificant and meaningless.

As I lie here, waiting for my death, these conflicting feelings well up in me. I am alone, with only my hospice nurse and housekeeper present. I finally found the answers I so desperately was looking for, but it is too late for me; my life is over. I am determined though, to leave something behind so my life was not completely lived in vain. I, therefore, am writing this book, so others will hopefully learn these important lessons and take the time before they die to experience life as it is meant to be lived.

Do Not Waste Your Life Living in Fear

If we measure time from the beginning of the universe, our life passes like a grain of sand on a beach or a drop of water in an ocean. To waste our brief life living in fear, believing we are better than another, accepting the self-centered myths we have been taught about our importance in the world, masks the true purpose of life.

To live a truly meaningful life, we must ignore everything we have been taught and believed to be true about our importance in the world; accepting, though we are all different, our life is not that significant. Every life, regardless of our differences, accomplishments, or genus, each with a spirit, a piece of god within, is, and always has been, as important as another's.

Part 3

B odhi is revealing everything to me so quickly, I barely have time to understand what he is saying. He is telling me why we are born; it surprises me how simple his message is. There have been many who have sought the answer to this question throughout the ages, yet so few who have found it. Bodhi is telling me about awakening, enlightenment, the meaning of life, and so much more, as well as what is preventing everyone from understanding and achieving each of these milestones in their lives. To understand these things, we need to take down the veil masking the answers we seek. By doing so, we can accept the possibility we have always had all the answers; we were only looking for them in the wrong place. To find these answers, to awaken, become enlightened, and find meaning in our life, I now understand the answers lie within each of us, where they have always been.

I think it is important to not only understand this, but also know what life can be like if this change happens to you. Though my time now is rapidly fading and is very precious, I must take at least a few minutes to tell you about this.

Imagine pure joy, love, happiness, and empathy for all life, living in a world where there is no fear or hate, only love. There is a sadness present as well, though this sadness arises from seeing everyone else believing the illusions life teaches us as we are growing up and the consequences of believing these illusions are real.

We fall into Anatta's trap. Look at the world we are living in, and the results of believing these illusions become obvious. War, death, hunger, homelessness, fear, hate, greed, prejudice, selfishness, climate change, and so much more are evident in every part of our world. None of these things need happen if only we all understood what I do now. Imagine what the world could be like if we were to change the paradigm and live our lives with love rather than fear.

I am 85 years old and today I am going to die. It is strange when you realize the end is so near. As I lie in my bed, waiting for the end of my life, I am alone; Anatta has little to say. There was no more advice from her now on how to be happy. No longer did she tell me I was better than everyone else because I was famous and had a lot of money. I finally began to realize none of that mattered at all. I will lie in my coffin alone, just as I had been alone all my life.

Instead, Bodhi, who I had rarely heard since I was born, has my undivided attention today. Just as before I was born, when only he was present, he has much to say before I will die. He tells me about the mask and the wall Anatta created to protect me and how these prevented him from helping me or being heard throughout my life. He also tells me I was never better than anyone else and no one's life is superior to another, regardless of wealth, race, gender, or anything else.

I began to remember everything Bodhi had taught me before I was born. I remember he had told me what the meaning of life was, and I began to realize how I had failed to follow his advice while I was alive. Bodhi was very understanding, though, telling me he would return with me to be reborn once more, so I could try to learn the lessons I was unable to learn during this life.

As I began to reflect on everything that had happened while I was alive, I also began to understand what a failure my entire life was. As I examine my life today, I am realizing almost everything Anatta told me was wrong and untrue. Throughout my adult life, I was beautiful and wealthy, yet now that I am about to die, none of that matters. I know when I die, my once beautiful body will wither away to dust.

What if I had never learned to wear a mask or imprison my spirit behind the wall Anatta built? What if my authentic self was able to shine its light brightly for all the world to see? I wonder how different my life could have been. Today, on the day I am going to die, I can finally answer these questions.

To live in a world where your light brightly shines and is freely given to others brings incredible inner peace. This peace is shared, as is all our resources, to assure every life has an equal chance to experience and find the meaning of life as well. The depression and loneliness I felt every day of my life, would no longer haunt me, being replaced instead by compassion and love. No longer would I feel lonely, as my love would not only be unconditionally shared by Bodhi, but by all others in which a spirit guide exists as well. I would finally understand what I sought is not found in the many distractions in the world, but only by sharing selflessly with others. If my wall and mask were never there, I would have been able to meditate, closing my eyes, quieting my mind, listening, and finally being able to hear Bodhi, rather than keeping so busy I never would have time to hear his message.

On this last day of my life, everything was obvious. My only wish was I would have known this much earlier in my life, to make amends for the selfishness that was to dictate every single day I was alive. If I would have known what I know today, I would have slowed down, not worked as much, taken the time to be with those most important to me, and shared my love with all I was blessed to have met throughout my life.

I would have gotten to know my children and spent time with them as they were growing up. Instead of focusing only my career and happiness and leaving their care to a nanny, I would have shared my love with them as well. I would have worked less and would have thus had memories of both their good and bad times. I would have also been there for them as a mentor, to direct them onto the spiritual path rather than the worldly path that I, and so many others, follow through life. I would have done many things so differently if only I had known what I know today.

My life appeared to go by so slowly this day, almost in slow motion, as I waited to take my last breath. Not only did every event in my life flash before me, but Bodhi also had a lot of time to talk with me. This is the story Bodhi told me. It is a story I have heard before while I waited to be born within my mother's womb, though I do not remember hearing it before today.

A spirit guide is universal; it is present within all living things. It is also eternal and will never die. Its job is to help others in their journey through life. They exist throughout the universe, as life exists on many of the planets throughout the billions of known galaxies in the universe. As I was to discover today, we are not alone and never have been. Life is far more complex and diverse than we ever thought.

The spirit guide exists to assist us to make choices that will help us understand lessons we are supposed to learn while we are alive. Though this may appear to be an easy job, it is not. Its voice is often dimmed and muted by the realities of trying to survive in the world after we are born. Its message is simple though: it is a message of love given without expectation. By sharing its love with others, life becomes much easier and meaningful; we each become stronger when we combine our essence together.

Imagine if we all shared this essence with each other, how the world would not only be transformed but changed forever. By doing this, assuring every life is respected, love would finally dominate fear and the true meaning of life would finally be revealed. Instead of living in a self-centered, greedy, selfish competitive world as we do now, we would live in a world in which selflessness and compassion reign. In this world, everything would be shared equally. There would no longer be homelessness, and no one would be dying from starvation or treatable illnesses. There would also no longer be hate, fear, or war since greed and inequality would no longer be present. Not only would everyone be recognized as equal, with no one considered better than another, but the importance of every life would be recognized as well. Compassion and selfless love would finally dominate life, as it was meant to be.

Bodhi is telling me, on our world, we are rapidly approaching a crossroads where we need to choose between evolving or extinction. To evolve, many of us will need to accept the spirit's message of universal love and denounce greed, hate, and fear. By doing this, a Darwinian evolution will hopefully result, in which those who do not accept this view of life will become extinct. If, however, we are unable to do this, then the disappearance of all life on this planet may very well be the result we settle for.

With the veil hiding the truth from me being lifted, I now understood what life is supposed to be like when the many distractions of the world no longer influence me. I never even considered or imagined this was possible, but I am assured by Bodhi it is. The possibilities I see is a world of peace, light, and love, rather than a world of war, darkness, and hate. My entire life, I believed the latter was all there was because it was all I knew, read about, and saw as I traveled around the world; I know I am not alone in this assumption.

To me, it appeared most of us not only believed this to be true, but also accepted the reality nothing could be done to change it. From the time we were little, as we learned what the world was really like, we blindly accepted and became insensitive to these negative emotions and events as we watched and read about it, saw it on tv, in movies, and on the internet. It became normal to watch others suffer and die. If it was a good movie, we could watch hundreds of people die; their lives apparently having very little value or meaning. After a while, we became numb to seeing this, to the point when it happened in real life, it had little effect on us. I remember, after seeing one of these tragedies happen in real life, though I felt bad, I simply went on with my life, not giving it a second thought.

As I lie here today, on my last day of life, I wonder how my life may have been different if I had embraced living in a world of peace, rather than one of endless violence. And I wonder how different the world would be if we all embraced this radical shift in our paradigm. I lie here imagining living in a world where there was no war, famine, hatred, or fear, where our concern is for each other, rather than just for ourselves. A world where compassion and love mean no one is hungry, homeless, or dies needlessly; here, greed would no longer dominate our lives, being replaced instead by love. I began to understand all this and much more; I knew we could change everything today, if only we had the will to do so. The technology exists now to eliminate these scourges from our planet. The only thing preventing this is the greed and selfishness of those who consider wealth more important than people.

I am writing this book today to let you know what I finally understand about life. It is my hope, even though my life was a complete failure and lived without meaning, you will not make the same mistakes and choices I did. I pray, by sharing my story, some good may yet come from my life, motivating you to be the change needed to live a fulfilling life and, by doing so, build the utopian world Bodhi describes, even if it only comes on the last day I am alive.

The Matrix

The matrix is a world where most are asleep, living in a learned reality accepted as the truth. Those who remain sleeping throughout their lives believe success, happiness, and meaning may be found in the self-centered world; they may not.

When we first awaken, we start to question if those beliefs are true. Despite how successful our life has been, sensing a voice we begin to hear within, the self-centered beliefs we once unquestionably accepted as the truth no longer make sense to us.

The matrix we once understood and accepted as our reality begins to dissolve, leaving an unrecognizable world in its place. Rather than compete against each other to survive in the world, we now wish to selflessly help others instead. Open your heart, see the genuine possibility's life offers, allowing your matrix to melt away.

Chapter 10
Reviewing My Life and Regrets

L

ife is funny and ironic. My parents named me Rue, which means regret, and as I lie here waiting to die, I now realize I had lived my entire life full of regrets.

Though I knew many people, had three children, four ex-husbands, was famous, and had fans all over the world, I felt totally alone. I took several medications, saw a counselor every week for my severe depression, and, though these may have helped me a bit, I still considered ending my life so the pain I felt within would finally go away. The only constant in my life, since I was a child, was the paralyzing emotional pain, sadness, and depression I have always felt: a pain coming from my very core.

My entire life, I felt like I was playing a role, as if life was simply a play. When I was working, I was an actress, acting and pretending to be someone else. As I found out today, the rest of my life, when I was not acting, I was playing a role as well. It turns out life is simply one big play.

I was to find out, on the last day of my life, I simply had a small role in this play. I always believed the goal of life was to be successful, become wealthy, and enjoy life. To accomplish this, I would travel, party, buy nice things, and have a good time. I never realized, though, how untrue this was.

It appears to me now the opposite is true. The happiest people I had met in my life were Salama and her family in Africa. They had very few material possessions or money, though their emotions and understanding about life were pure and real. They truly understood life far better than I did and, though I made a lot of money being an actress, they were far wealthier than I was. Until today, I never understood this; now, it is very clear to me.

What I am learning today is as surprising to me as it may be to each of you. Little that happened in my life was real or true. Though everything that happened was predestined, I had made choices throughout my life which would determine the direction it would go. If only I had understood this earlier,

I could have made many different choices. However, I accepted, as most of us do, the easy path by following the advice from Anatta. The alcohol and drugs I took since I was 12 years old dulled the pain I was feeling within, so I did not have to face the reality of my true feelings. I, of course, did not know any of this. Since I had imprisoned Bodhi within my heart when I was 7 years old, I never was able to feel or know my real emotions.

This explains why I was such a good actress; I had been acting my entire life. I was better than most; I won many awards throughout my life for my acting skill and prowess. I was proud of my abilities, never realizing how they were truly affecting my life. But I realize now that life is not real; it is a play, in which we all have our bit roles.

Though we do have choices as to how we project ourselves during our lives and the direction our life will take, those leading to discovering our authentic-self are difficult to discover. They are hidden deep within each of us, behind the façade we project for the other actors in the play. It is difficult to penetrate the façade or change our lines in the play, but it is not impossible.

We each have choices we make throughout our life allowing us to make these changes; the question is do we have the strength of will to do so. It is far easier to follow the status quo, not confronting our mask and wall; doing so means confronting the demons we have within when they were first created. It is only by ripping off our mask and shattering our wall we may truly discover the play we are acting in is not real and the direction our life has taken us has led to our unhappiness. If we can do this, the emotions we finally will feel and share will be real, and the direction of our life will lead to inner peace and a true understanding of life's purpose.

In my role as an actress, I got to travel all over the world and see many things. But there were two essential things I noticed, regardless of what country I was working in or continent I was on: how similar everyone was and how vicious and mean we can be not only each other but to all life.

Regardless of their religion, culture, ethnicity, or anything else, everyone primarily seeks love and happiness. I always thought the only way to achieve both was by having a lot of money. Today, I realize this was not true. Just as Salama and her family appeared to be both happy and sincerely have love for each other, so did many others I met around the world. This was true not only in Africa, but also Asia, South America, and other places I worked and visited.

I saw many living in poverty, struggling to survive. Though our cultures may have been quite different, the goals we had, to find happiness and love, were the same.

I also learned our ability to kill, hurt, and lack compassion for each other and all life on our planet is endless. When I was making a movie in Africa in the early 1990s, there was a civil war in the neighboring nation of Rwanda. There, more than 500,000 Tutsi were slaughtered by the majority Hutu government. Many of those were killed by machetes and the victims were not only men, but also women and children.

I also read about the Chinese genocide led by communist leader Mao Ze-Dong, in which over 50 million people were killed, over 6 million Jews killed in concentration camps by Hitler during WWII, the many deaths of Native Americans in North America, and so many other genocides in which humanity's inhumanity for its own was exposed. Such senseless violence, for what? All these people died because of greed, politics, religion, hate, prejudice, and fear.

Today, on the day I am going to die, as I am reliving my life, I remember all this and much more. I was famous; I had the opportunity to bring light to many of these atrocities I saw and read about and to help others less fortunate than I was, yet I did nothing. I surrendered to my apathy as I focused on myself. I wasted my life, worrying what others thought and what was best for me. I dulled my senses every day using drugs and alcohol. I did not even have time to sincerely care about those who were closest to me, my family. Rather than spend time with them, I isolated myself from them as well.

Today, on the last day of my life, I finally understand the mask and wall, both fashioned when I was just a small child, and the profound effect they were to have on me throughout my life. They were so effective, not only were those closest to me not able to penetrate them, but I was not able to either. Though I tried to show love to my family, the love I was able to show was learned, superficial. As I am discovering today, it was not authentic love, love we are inherently born with residing within our heart.

As I lie here alone, waiting to die, my life flashes before me in slow motion. I finally understand, though I was successful, how unimportant and insignificant my life was. Though I was famous and owned many nice things, it no longer mattered. For the first time, I look back at those I met throughout my life, who were not as lucky as I was, and wonder if perhaps they were more fortunate and wealthier than I.

As I lie here waiting to die, Bodhi describes what living in an enlightened world is like. This utopian world Bodhi is describing to me seems impossible, but he assures me it is not. What is needed for this to happen is a shift in consciousness. We must challenge everything we are taught and learn throughout our life, renouncing the ideology of competition and self-interest, replacing it with universal concern and selfless love for everyone instead. The false paths we learn to follow as we are growing up lead us to believe and accept a skewed view of life: a view where competition and loneliness dominate, rather than our natural inherent instincts of cooperation, compassion, and love we are born with.

To find the right path in life, we must unlearn almost everything we learned and believed to be true as we were growing up. How hard could that be? As I was to find out, it is an extremely difficult thing to do. It was not until today, 85 years after I was born, I was to finally able to understand this. I wish I could have more time to experience this feeling, knowing what I do today; or to have found out about it much earlier in my life. But, like so many of us, who only learn about this on the last day of our life, when Anatta releases her hold on us, it is too late for me now.

As I lie here waiting to die, I have many regrets. I am therefore writing this book in the hope others will learn what I have just remembered today, and it will not be too late to change the direction of their life before the day they are going to die.

Is There a Reason We Are Alive?

After we are born, some may begin to wonder why they are alive. Is it just to survive, succeed, and enjoy our life, idly passing time until we get old and die? If we make a lot of money, own many nice possessions, have a family, or anything else many would say is our reason for life, when we prepare to die, would we feel our life was successful, important, and worthwhile?

Or is there more to our journey through life than just what we were told? Most remain asleep, going through the motions, passing time, doing the many mundane things life offers until they die. There are others, though, who begin to question if perhaps there is more to life, beginning to sense within an unrelenting message, waking them from their deep slumber.

When this happens they begin to reevaluate everything they once believed to be true. The choice which path in life we each take is ours; we may alter our choice at any time. By silently listening, in between our racing thoughts, to the innate wisdom and unconditional loving messages of our spirit within, the genuine reason we are alive will become evident.

Chapter 11
A Second Chance

A

bout four hours before I am to die, something extraordinary happened. My three children came to say goodbye to me. I was in tears; this was the best gift I had ever been given. I did not want to die alone. I spent my entire life worrying only about myself and because of this, I had neglected my children and they resented me for it. Though I did not realize it at the time, I had wasted my entire life pursuing my own happiness in the world, instead of sharing the love a parent should instinctively have for their children and for everyone else.

How can someone, surrounded by people all the time, be totally alone? The mask and the wall allowed no one, not even my three children or four ex-husbands, to get to know the real me. All they or anyone else saw was the artificial facade I had learned to project when I was a young child. The love I tried to show was learned in the world from what I had imagined love was like; it did not come from my heart, where my spirit and authentic love are.

I blindly followed the path I learned throughout my life, as most of us do: the path of the false prophet Anatta. This path led me to believe the answers to life may only be found by finding success in the world and that this success would be defined by society. As I found out today, nothing could be further from the truth.

If we live to an old age, as I did, does that mean we have lived a successful life? Is that the meaning of life? I know today it is not. It is not how long you live that is important; rather, it is the quality of your life. Someone may live just 10 years yet have a more meaningful life than another who lived to old age. What is important is what you believe in and do with your time that will determine if your life was important and had meaning, not how long you were alive.

Today, on the day I am to die, without all the distractions of the world and Anatta's control over my life, I finally understand everything I had done looking for happiness was wrong. All the work, partying, traveling, drugs, and alcohol were only distractions. With only Bodhi's voice present now, I can see the answers clearly.

I now realize happiness and meaning in life cannot be found in the world where I was looking for it, but rather must be found within. Only by ripping off the mask we wear and shattering the wall isolating each of us from others and ourselves can our true inherent emotions and feelings be revealed. The meaning of life will only be found by destroying the barriers we artificially erect, allowing us to find the selfless love existing within. Only by sharing this love with all others will true and lasting happiness be found.

I had bought the illusion of life by believing my happiness and success in the world would be determined by money, looks, and material possessions, rather than accepting my spirit's message of selfless love. Suddenly, everything began to make sense. On this day, without Anatta's constant noise and barrage of misinformation, what I had been searching for my entire life, inner peace, and love, was finally revealed to me. I only wish I had heard and understood it many years ago.

As I lie in my bed, waiting for death to end the pain, depression, and loneliness I had felt my entire life, I was finally able to ask my children for their forgiveness. I never realized or accepted before today the many problems we had were my fault. I always found a way to blame everyone else for my problems, especially those closest to me. With tears streaming down my face, I begged my children for their forgiveness. The greatest gift in life I ever received happened that very moment, with my three children standing around me, smiling, telling me they understood, forgave, and loved me as well. Immediately, a weight, that bore me down my entire life, was lifted. For the first time in my life, I felt true love and joy. There was no more pretense, only the real emotions and knowledge of all Bodhi had once taught me.

Just before my last breath, my entire life flashed before me. Though it may have only lasted a few minutes at the most, to me it seemed like hours or days. Everything that happened to me throughout my life replayed in my mind, as if in slow motion. I saw myself inside my mother, loved and content, waiting to be born. Life was so simple and easy then. It was the first time I met Bodhi and was the only time, except for right now, I could hear his messages clearly.

I relived when Anatta and I were being born almost simultaneously and the many things we learned together throughout our life. I saw my mask forming, covering my entire face, and my wall being built around my heart, imprisoning Bodhi within.

I saw every experience I had and every person I met. I understood the many mistakes I made during my life and how I had chosen the wrong path in life to follow. It was too late for me to change anything now, but I finally understood the path Anatta had led me down, the path I followed throughout my life, led to the sadness, depression, and anxiety I experienced every day. I also understood, if I had only followed the path Bodhi wanted me to, my life would have been different and meaningful.

I understood all this in just the last few moments of my life. It is my hope you will discover this truth much sooner than I.

Forgiveness

When we harm another in any manner, we may cause them enduring pain. It matters not if the injury is emotional, physical, verbal, or in any other form. The hurt we caused is always wrong, requiring pardon to the one we injured. Though we may believe we are justified in our actions, they never are.

Do not let our imperfect humanity, our ego, allow the wrong to happen or for us not to sincerely apologize if it has already occurred. Only by correcting our human indiscretions, will we be able to awaken, allowing us to begin a quest to discover our true purpose in life.

Chapter 12
The Afterlife

A fter I died, something surprising happened. I was not religious at all while I was alive, so I was pleasantly surprised to find death was not the end. I died at 7 o'clock in the evening, just as the sun was drifting below the mountain top and dusk was setting in. I was grateful my children were by my side; I, therefore, did not have to be alone when I took my last breath. Though I had struggled throughout my life, I was finally at peace; my children had forgiven me, and I now understood the reason I was born.

I realized, just before the moment of my death, I had wasted my entire life, searching throughout the world for what I already possessed within my heart. The many struggles, unhappiness, loneliness, and depression I felt throughout my life happened because I was looking for my answers in the wrong place. I had bought into the illusion of life. I had lived my life and acted my part in the play so well, until the last day I was alive, I never even realized it was a play at all and none of it was real.

At the moment of my death, Bodhi left my body, leaving Anatta behind with the shell she had lived in for the past 85 years. Bodhi told me when we die, both our body and Anatta die as well; only the spirit is eternal. After death, the spirit moves to a different plane of existence, at a higher frequency in the universe, where there are others like it. Without Anatta's influence, all I felt in this new plane of existence was unconditional love. Everything Bodhi had taught me so very long ago, within my mother's womb before I was born, clearly returned now, as if it had been yesterday. I also remembered how naïve I was at that time, thinking how easy Bodhi's message was to understand; sharing love selflessly was the answer to the question we all will seek to find after we are born, the answer to the meaning of life. Little did I know then the influence Anatta was to have on me and on all living things.

Before I discuss more what the afterlife is like, it is important to understand what is necessary for you to remain there after you die. Life can really be broken down into four stages: we are conceived, we are born, we live our life, and we die. Before we are born and after we die, we only know the spirit guide. It is when we are alive many challenges are presented to each of us. Specifically, the challenges I am talking about all revolve around the ego or self. To evolve and remain in the afterlife, it is necessary, by the end of your life, to travel the path your spirit guide has laid out for you.

For those who have not successfully traveled this path, they will need to return to seek this knowledge once more. If you cannot find this path or if you have not yet evolved enough to have traveled far enough down the path your spirit guide wishes you to take, you will be destined to return, as many times as necessary, until you are able to.

The word acceptance is important here as many awaken during their journey and begin to travel the spirit guide's path. Unless you fully accept what you have learned though, your journey will never be complete. Earlier, I had talked about the difference between an awakening and enlightenment. I will now tell you what it is. An awakening is knowing, realizing a spirit exists within all life, but the self still dominates our lives. At this point, you still get caught up in the everyday mundane issues life presents.

Enlightenment, however, is the acceptance of what you have learned. When one becomes enlightened, your life is now dominated by the spirit. Though the self/ego will always remain while you are alive, the direction your life will follow will now be dictated by your spirit instead. When you reach this point, you become enlightened, and the lessons on this plane of existence will no longer need to be repeated.

In the afterlife, there were many others like me who never learned this lesson until it was too late, on the day we were going to die. For us, we were destined to return once more to try to internalize our spirit's messages of hope and love; the cycle of life would be repeated. A spirit guide would once again be asked to join a new life within a mother's womb, meeting Anatta after it was born, to live life again.

The rest, however, who had found the answers, awakened, and became enlightened during their last journey through life, were blessed to move to a new plane of existence. This was where their spirit would join others like them, existing as one.

The many challenges we face in life are multifold and diverse. There are several reasons though, why we are here to face those challenges. Some say it is destiny, karma, or that our lives are preordained. Others believe we are born to learn certain things allowing us to move to a higher plane of existence. If those lessons are learned, then you will be able to merge with others like you. It is only after we accept the spirit's path and teachings during our lifetime this may be accomplished. Only then will all the lessons have been learned and the meaning of life become clear. It is here, on the next plane of existence, our true destiny lies. Hopefully, I will choose the right path in life with my next incarnation.

In a religious sense, this plane of existence is where heaven is. god is the combination, the totality, of all life once alive who awoke and became enlightened during their last journey through life and now exist together as one. In this scenario, heaven is where enlightened spirits exist together, and god is the combination, the totality, of many billions of enlightened lives existing before and continuing to exist together as one in peace and harmony.

In this idealistic plane of existence, there are no negative emotions; there is no fear, hate, anger, prejudice, inequality, or anything else confusing us as it did while we were alive; there is only love. Since Anatta only exists while we are alive, everything associated with her has no meaning here. There are only spirits here, emanating unconditional love. The atmosphere reflects the peace and love many of us sought but never found during our life. What prevented us from finding it was Anatta; but of course, we did not know that at the time.

I'm sure you are wondering what a spirit looks like, since we have not talked about that yet. spirits are pure energy and cannot be seen by the naked eye. Their individual presence exists though, outlined by an energy force surrounding their essence within. As they encounter others like them, their strength increases exponentially.

One of the greatest surprises I had, before having to leave the afterlife to be reborn again, was that there were spirit guides from throughout the galaxies. How naïve I was to think life only existed on our little insignificant planet. As I was to discover, there are at least 100 billion galaxies in the known universe, each one containing billions upon billions of stars. Each one of those stars may have multiple planets in orbit around them. This means there are likely many trillions of planets in the universe.

With all these planets, to believe life did not exist anywhere else is truly unthinkable; and it was. The number of other worlds these spirit guides came from were too numerous to count, but interestingly, their purpose was the same, regardless of where they came from. They were there to help others in their journey through life as well. Just as a spirit guide joins each of us through our life, they also joined each life form from the many inhabited planets in the universe. I wondered, when I returned, if I would reincarnate on earth or perhaps on another planet. And then, if I take things even one step further, since a spirit guide exists within all living things, including animals and plants, I wondered if I would return as a dominant life form or as something else. I guess I will just have to wait to find out.

Why Are We Alive?

Numerous philosophers, religious leaders, and many others have attempted to answer the question: why are we alive? The best answer I have found is: we are alive to reunite with our spirit within, then share its infinite wisdom and unconditional love with all others.

Any other explanation is a deception, fostered by the ego, our learned beliefs, to make our life's journey more challenging.

Epilogue

I had been depressed my entire life. Despite taking anti-depressant medications and frequent counseling sessions, my depression continued unabated. Today, as I lie waiting to die, I finally came to know and understand the underlying cause of my depression. I only wish the cause was found many years earlier.

As I lay waiting to die, I am going to take a few of the precious moments I have left to talk to the professionals who try to help others with depression, anxiety, and other psychological and medical problems. My advice is to put away your textbooks and everything you learned. Instead, open your mind to other possibilities.

There is a place for traditional psychology and medical treatments of illnesses, though treatment must not stop there. If the spiritual part of an illness is not equally treated, the help you are giving others is only partial and temporary.

Everything we have talked about in my life should give you pause to consider the possibility's life offers. From our spirit, Anatta (our ego), understanding the meaning of life, the possibility of an afterlife and everything else affecting us throughout our lives should give you, the reader, much to think about. It is my hope, by writing this book, you may enrich your thinking and consider following a different path.

After hearing my story, think how much is lost by not considering the spiritual component to life when treating illnesses. Just as the depression, loneliness, and unhappiness in my life was never completely treated because the spiritual part of my life was not even considered, imagine what might have been different for me and so many others if it had. Though many will deny it vigorously, there is a spiritual aspect to life having a profound effect on each of us. By ignoring this possibility much will be lost.

Today, on the day I am going to die, I finally understood my entire life was a play; it was all make-believe. I acted my part so well I never knew it was not real. Life is an illusion, where we all have our bit parts in the play. If we follow the script, as we are told, the answers we seek about life may elude you as well.

It is only when we ad-lib, act outside the boundaries of the script, the answers we seek may finally reveal themselves. If we do this, however, the path may be lonely and difficult. Many of our family and friends will not understand our choice. It is important to take this path anyway and share this knowledge with everyone you can. If we do, the possibilities are endless, for our future and the future of all life on this planet depend on this.

The world today, and throughout history, is a very harsh egocentric place to live in. It is full of fear, hate, anger, greed, and selfishness leading to war, murder, hunger, and homelessness. Unfortunately, these lists of maladies could go on almost in perpetuity. If we continue down this path of destruction, there is only one possible outcome: extinction.

We have a choice to make, but it must be made very soon: to continue to follow our self-destructive ways or to choose an entirely new path, one embracing love over fear. If we choose love, then instead of the aforementioned destructive emotions, there will be compassion, sharing, and empathy as we help each other succeed in life. We have the technology now, to eliminate these scourges; all we lack is the will, compassion, and selflessness to do so.

As I was to discover, on the last day of my life, there is a reason we are alive, a meaning to life. We can either continue to ignore the reason and be destined to remain on our destructive path or we can embrace the true meaning of life, which is to help each other succeed by sharing our unconditional love selflessly. No one, not one single person, in which a spirit is also present, should be ignored or left out.

Is success in life defined by the prestige of our job or the amount of money we make or is it defined by the content of our character and selflessness of our love? That is a question we must all ask ourselves. Unfortunately, if we continue down the former path, nothing will change; and just like the many species of animals and plants, in which a spirit also exists, have become extinct under humankind's dominance, we too will follow them into oblivion.

Do we really believe we are so special this cannot or will not happen to us? If, as I was to discover, there is life on many of the trillions of other planets in the universe, will our species even be missed? We have been given a gift; whether we continue to squander it is a critical choice we must make. With the threat of nuclear war, climate change, and so much more, it appears the time to make this decision is rapidly approaching.

Do we really want to continue to live in the world as it is today, a world of hate, fear, and concern only for ourselves; or are we ready to choose the alternative? We all have a choice to make; it is my hope we choose wisely.

The Mind, Body, Spirit Connection

Psychologists and counselors enable us to return and function in society, but often, their two-dimensional approach, treating only the mind and body, is deficient and inadequate.

Without also treating the spiritual part of an illness, the treatment is incomplete. The spirit gives our lives meaning. When it is ignored, the result is simply a return to mediocrity.

Author's Note:

It is my hope your understanding of awakening, enlightenment, and spirituality has been enhanced by reading 'Today I Am Going to Die', book 1 of 'The Awakening Tetralogy'. If it has, could you please take a few minutes to: "Write a Review" and recommend this book on social media and to your friends and family.

The Awakening Tetralogy was written to try to awaken and help others who are awakened more fully understand what enlightenment is, so their spiritual journey through life may be more fully realized.

Thank you for taking the time to read:

Today I Am Going to Die. Please consider reading the other three books in this series as well.

Thank you so much for reading 'Today I Am Going to Die'. I am including an addendum with an assortment of 50 spiritual reflections using metaphor, imagery, and spiritual insight to explore themes of awakening, enlightenment, and the human pursuit of meaning. These spiritual reflections are included in Book 2 of Our Search for Meaning. It is my hope you may consider reading the three books in this series as well, as you further your search to discover the meaning of life.

Books by Ken Luball

The four Spiritual books in The Awakening Tetralogy:
Today I Am Going to Die: Choices in Life
The Spirit Guide: Journey Through Life
Tranquility: A Village of Hope
The Illusion of Happiness: Choosing Love Over Fear
A Mystical Trilogy: 'Our Search for Meaning' - a series of three books of thoughtful easily understandable spiritual reflections about awakening, enlightenment, spirituality, & the meaning of life.

A Spiritual Duology: '*Spiritual Reflections*' - Two books of spiritual reflections using metaphor, imagery, and spiritual insight to explore themes of awakening, enlightenment, and the human pursuit of meaning.

The first three stories in *The Awakening Tetralogy* are written in the first person, following the spiritual journey through life of a child, as they learn the lessons needed during their life to awaken and become enlightened. These books are written in an understandable, interesting, unique narrative, which is both thought-provoking and engaging.

To find links for each of these nine books please visit my website: kenluball.com[1].

ADDENDUM:

SPIRITUAL

REFLECTIONS

Glossary

<u>Asleep</u> – After we are born we are taught how to survive in the world and what success is. We therefore learn to worry only about our own success and survival in the world, rather than to be concerned about others. This results in living in a self-centered world of prejudice, inequity, and endless struggle. Those who fully believe this are asleep, accepting the status quo as the truth.

<u>Awaken</u> – There may come a time in our life when, despite our success in the world, we begin to question the truth of our self-centered learned beliefs, our ego. When this happens the first quiet messages of the spirit, a piece of god present within every life are sensed, beginning us on an enduring journey to discover meaning in our life.

<u>Ego</u> – The ego is everything we learn, believe, and accept is true after we are born, as we learn how to survive in a self-centered world. Its primary concern is what is best for us; it worries little about others. It also attempts to build up our self-esteem by convincing us of our value in the world.

<u>Enlightenment</u> – The complete acceptance of the spiritual path, allowing the spirit's inherent wisdom and unconditional love to be our primary guide in life. With enlightenment, the ego, our self-centered learned beliefs, assumes a secondary role in our life, no longer influencing the direction of our life choices.

<u>Spirit/ Soul/ God / Higher-Self</u> – An ethereal entity accompanying and inextricably connecting every life to another's. Its purpose is to give our lives meaning by sharing its inherent wisdom and unconditional love to help guide our life's choices.

<u>Spirituality</u> – Spirituality is the belief there is a piece of god, a spirit or soul within every life intimately linking each of us to the other, and, because of this, each life, regardless of our differences, accomplishments, or genus, is important, equal, and connected.

The Mountain Top

Surrounded by towering white
   covered peaks, the snow begins
   to melt in spring.
   Its water flows, rippling past rocks
   downhill in streams, sustaining
   the many forest inhabitants.
   To reach the mountain summit,
   an arduous climb is required; sheer
   rock cliffs, high winds, freezing
   temperatures, present themselves
   as the mountain top is near.
   We begin our lives on top of the
   mountain with spectacular views
   of the world below.
   As we are taught about life
   though, and what is expected of
   us, our view begins to diminish;
   we begin to descend the mountain
   as we accept the truth of
   what we learned growing up.
   By the time we reach the base of
   The mountain, accepting all of
   society's self-centered viewpoints,
   we have forgotten what the beautiful
   scenic view on the peak looked like.
   We may only begin to reclimb the
   mountain when we begin to question
   if what we had learned and accepted
   during our lives was true.
   Once we realize and acknowledge
   little of it was, we may once again
   be able to reach the summit, and

appreciate the beautiful views
of the world below, as we
were always meant to do.

The Sword and the Shield

We are born free, though as
    we are exposed to the world
    and its beliefs, we each acquire
    a sword and a shield to protect
    us from life's injustices.
Our shield deflects injurious
    rage, preventing others words
    and deeds from hurting us.
Our sword is our response,
    as its sharp blade attempts to
    penetrate another's defenses.
These self-centered tools
    prevent us from ever
    discovering genuine love
    and meaning in our lives.
Only by yielding, putting down
    our instruments of conflict, will
    our true purpose in life
    become evident.
With this surrender, though our
    learned beliefs will remain, they
    will no longer direct our actions.
Rather, our spirit present within
    each life, free from its confines
    behind our sword and shield,
    will now be permitted to
    reveal our true destiny.

Our Sixth Sense

Most people imagine and
    live their entire lives believing
    there are only five senses: hearing,
    touch, sight, taste, and smell.
    Those who do, though they may
    have led a good life and been
    successful, have neglected the
    most important sense, our
    sixth sense: the spirit.
    Also known as soul, god, our
    higher-self, it opens life to a
    whole new dimension of thought,
    beliefs, and understanding.
    Our sixth sense permits us to
    find genuine meaning in our
    lives by allowing us to
    discover and selflessly
    share our loving core present
    within every life.
    Doing so is the reason we
    are born, the true meaning
    of our life's journey.

The Comfort of Silence

When we see a wrong, do or
    say nothing, we are contributing
    to the decline of our world.
    Many have different opinions
    as to what is considered wrong.
    Spiritually, morally, and ethically,
    wrong is doing anything to
    harm another in any way.
    It matters not if the injury is
    physical, verbal, or ignoring
    the many human offenses
    we inflict on each other.
    War, hunger, homelessness;
    prejudice, inequity, hate.
    These and many more human
    transgressions are caused by
    our comfort of silence, fearful
    of saying something to
    upset the status quo.
    We must be silent no more.
    Every indiscretion must be
    met and challenged with
    resistance, speaking up loudly
    in defense of those being harmed.
    If we see anything we would not
    wish to happen to us or those
    we are closest to, that is the
    measure to be silent no more.

Our Second Act

There may come a time in
our lives when we begin to
reevaluate everything we
once believed important.
Despite living a successful
life, having family, prestige,
money, material possessions,
a sense begins to emerge making
us question if there is more
to life than what we were
taught and achieved.
We awaken.
Often, this moment presents
an opportunity for our second
act in life to begin, as we
reevaluate our job, relationships,
beliefs, and everything else we
once believed to be true.
This feeling comes from our
spirit within and may cause
our lives to unravel as we
begin to question all
our choices in life.
Once we awaken, we may
never fall back asleep.
We begin to view the world
differently; one where we
realize our definition of
success was distorted.
Money, prestige, family, no
longer dominate our self-
centered view of the world.

Our second act in life begins
when we understand selflessly
helping others also find
success in the world is
the genuine reason
for our life's journey.

The Baker

I woke up at 3 a.m. every
    day for the past 45 years to
    prepare and bake cakes, bread,
    and other delicious pastries
    to sell in my bakery.
    I am now in the twilight of life.
    Where have all the years gone?
    As I sit on my porch, I
    begin to understand I spent
    those years working, buying
    things to make my life
    easier, paying bills.
    Is this all there is to life?
    If you answer yes, then,
    like me, our lives have
    not been fully lived.
    We simply went through
    the motions, doing everything
    we were taught to live
    a successful life.
    It is only now, as death nears,
    I finally understand there is
    so much more I was
    supposed to accomplish.
    I never genuinely knew love,
    inner peace, or happiness.
    Though I thought I did,
    had a family, traveled,
    did fun things, these
    emotions eluded me as

I only experienced
them superficially.
Though it is too late for
me, I now realize these
genuine emotions
have always been
part of me.
All I had to do to
experience them was
open my heart, then
selflessly share them
with others.
Perhaps if I had done
this, spent less time
burying my head in the
oven the pastries were
baked in, I would have
realized sooner, there
was so much more to life
than just doing what
I had been told.

The Storm

The darkening clouds
    above threaten the
    peaceful earth below.
    As the first drops of rain
    begin to fall, many race
    for shelter to avoid being
    caught in its wake.
    As the deluge increases,
    the howling wind intensifies
    the storms ferocity.
    Many barely notice the
    weather, safe, comfortable
    in their abode.
    There are others though,
    the discarded, the untouchables,
    ignored by society due to
    poverty or their life
    situation, who become
    drenched from the
    unrelenting wind and
    rain, having no shelter
    to protect them from
    the elements.
    An enlightened society
    would not allow anyone
    to stand alone in the storm.
    Rather, they would
    provide refuge to protect
    everyone, regardless of
    our differences or their

circumstances in life.
To truly change the world,
we must selflessly embrace
the outcasts, the discarded,
allowing them to find protection
from the storm as well.

A Long and Winding Road

There are many turns,
    curves, and detours we
    encounter on our
    journey through life.
    The final destination though,
    is the same: the reunification
    with our spirit, present
    within every life.
    How we get there is
    influenced by our
    experiences and acceptance
    of what we were taught and
    consider to be the truth.
    The more we believe our
    self-centered views are
    genuine, the sharper the
    turns in the road will be,
    making our journey
    longer, more challenging.
    For those who start to
    question these truths,
    beginning to sense a
    presence within, the
    turns and detours in
    the road lessen; its end
    may now become visible.
    Though few will reach
    the end of the road, it is
    the journey getting there
    that is life's true purpose.

What is the Purpose of the Spirit?

The spirit is an ethereal
    entity accompanying every
    life, present to share its
    inherent wisdom and
    unconditional love to
    allow our lives to have
    genuine meaning and purpose.
    The spirit may be considered
    to be our higher-self,
    a piece of god.
    It often is in competition
    with the self, our learned beliefs.
    Without the spirit, without
    striving to become one with
    our higher-self, all that is
    left are our experiences
    and survival techniques
    learned since we were born.
    Meaning found in a self-
    centered world is an illusion.
    It may only be discovered by
    accepting and selflessly
    sharing the wisdom and
    pure loving messages
    of the spirit within.

The Door

Imagine a hill with a
    door on the top.
    On one side of the hill,
    at its base, are our self-
    centered beliefs.
    When we are here, the
    hill is very steep and
    difficult to climb.
    As our spirit, the source
    of divine wisdom and
    intuition within us, becomes
    a little stronger, and we
    begin to awaken, the incline
    of the hill appears less severe;
    we may begin to ascend it
    in an effort to approach
    the door on the top.
    We know if we can reach
    the door and go through it,
    we will find enlightenment
    on the other side, becoming
    one with our higher-self.
    Though, at times, we may
    briefly pass through the door,
    the stress and anxieties
    of life soon return, and
    we find ourselves being
    dragged back through the
    door once more, falling
    back down the hill.

Only by fully embracing
the wisdom and unconditional
loving messages of our spirit
within, then selflessly sharing
them with others, may we
remain on the other side
of the door, and in doing
so, realize our true
purpose in life.

Chi (Qi)

Every life has two forms.
The physical form
is the body, mortal,
beginning at conception,
ending with death.
There is also essence
present within every life.
The essence is immortal,
joining each life in the
beginning and returning
to a higher vibrational
level when the body dies.
Though these appear to
be separate, chi is the
bridge connecting
them together.
Both will exist,
influencing us
throughout our brief life.
When our physical form,
with its emotions, thoughts,
and beliefs dominate, our
chi is weakened, often
resulting in stress,
hardship, and anxiety.
When our essence, however,
dominates, our future brightens.
To embrace the power,
the energy of our chi,
accept the spiritual path

through life, unleashing
the force of our spirit's
inherent wisdom and
unconditional love,
allowing us to begin
a journey to discover
our life's genuine purpose.

The Messages Within

We need not travel,
  amass material possessions,
  have a lot of money, or
  anything else that may
  be found in the world
  to find genuine
  happiness, meaning,
  love, and inner peace.
  Though many endlessly
  search for these in a self-
  centered world, they
  may not be found there.
  To discover where they
  truly exist, sit in a
  comfortable chair,
  silence your mind,
  listen to the quiet
  messages in between
  your racing thoughts,
  then selflessly share
  the wisdom and
  unconditional love you
  sense with the world.

Religious Divisions

Easter, Passover, Ramadan.
   Christian, Jewish, Muslim.
   These are but three of many
   religions dividing, rather
   than uniting the world.
   The differences have led
   to prejudice, wars,
   indifference to the
   struggles of those
   who believe differently.
   Though each may have
   differing views on god,
   the underlying message
   they voice has been lost.
   It is a message of unselfishly
   helping and loving others,
   guaranteeing the right of
   everyone to be safe, have
   food to eat, a home to live
   in, a planet that will not be
   destroyed by greed and apathy.
   It is treating every person,
   regardless of our beliefs,
   and all forms of life, with
   the same respect we wish
   for ourselves.
   Perhaps it is time to put
   our self-centered learned
   religious beliefs aside,
   embracing instead the

initial spiritual messages
Jesus, Moses, and Mohammed,
had originally intended
for us to adopt.
A message of unconditional
love, selflessly shared with
others, for the benefit of all.

The Barrier to Enlightenment

When we are awakened,
    we realize more than
    just the self is present
    and influencing us.
    We begin to understand
    the spirit exists as well.
    What prevents an
    awakened person from
    reaching enlightenment
    is this knowledge is
    not fully accepted.
    There is still a belief,
    fostered by the self,
    that meaning, happiness,
    and inner peace may be
    found in a self-centered
    world; it cannot.
    It must first be
    discovered within,
    then it must be shared
    without motive or
    benefit, with all others.

Our Higher-Self

The reason we are
    born, what our higher-
    self represents, is a
    return to the inherent
    knowledge and
    unconditional love
    present within every
    life before our birth,
    unimpeded by the
    distraction's life presents us.
    Our spirit teaches us to
    be selfless, loving,
    compassionate to
    everyone, regardless
    of our differences.
    It lets us know every
    life is equally important,
    and only by helping each
    other unselfishly will
    the struggles we may
    have after we are born
    lessen, and the genuine
    meaning of our life's
    journey be understood.

Every Life is Meaningful

With enlightenment,
   the disguises others
   wear fade away.
   The negativity of life
   wanes, seeing the best
   in others, rather than
   only their flaws.
   The desire to improve
   the world by helping
   others is overwhelming.
   With this understanding
   we realize every life is
   intimately connected by
   a spirit, a piece of god
   within, and each life
   therefore, regardless
   of our differences, has
   purpose and meaning.

The Irony of Life

When we are first
    born, we know only
    unconditional love.
    None of the harsh
    realities of the self-
    centered world have
    yet distorted our pure
    hopeful vision of life.
    With our socialization
    into the world though,
    we will never return to
    the innocence we once
    knew before our birth.
    The irony of life is we
    may then spend the rest
    of our lives undoing the
    damage done during our
    earliest years when our
    views, beliefs, prejudices,
    and opinions of the
    world are formed,
    trying desperately
    to return to the
    loving, peaceful
    moment we once
    knew before we
    were first born.

The Divide

Our world is endlessly
divided into castes.
Religion, ethnicity,
race, wealth, are just
a few of the many
divisions in a self-
centered world too
obsessed to notice
or care.
These division are used
to justify the superiority
of some over others.
They are also the primary
cause of war, prejudice,
inequity, and many of
humanity's other problems.
In spirituality there
are no castes.
Every life, though
different in appearance,
beliefs, genus, is equally
valuable, deserving to be
treated with respect and
unconditional love.
Only when this is
recognized and accepted,
may the spiritual evolution
of our planet finally begin.

The Reflection Pond

Look at yourself as
    you gaze into a calm
    pool of water; peer
    deeply into your eyes.
    Beyond the pretense,
    the façade we present
    to the world, a sentient
    being may be seen.
    Its purpose is to share
    its inherent knowledge
    and unconditional love
    with us, allowing our
    life to be led with true
    purpose and meaning.
    Only when we selflessly
    share this part of
    ourselves with others,
    will the genuine reason
    for our presence be
    truly understood.

Our True Path

From the moment
    we are born, with
    our first breath,
    everything changes.
    At that very instant,
    the ego, our self-centered
    beliefs, is created.
    Everything we see and
    are exposed to throughout
    our life will help
    strengthen the ego.
    Accepting what we are
    taught will be the cause
    of many challenges we
    may face and in allowing
    us to find true meaning
    in our life.
    We are born enlightened,
    with the inherent knowledge
    and unconditional love of
    the spirit, a piece of
    god within.
    It is not until we are
    socialized to accept the
    mores of society, we
    forget our true purpose.
    Everything we have
    learned from our birth
    are obstacles, encouraged
    by the ego, to detour us

from the genuine path
through life we are meant
to follow: the spiritual path.
With this understanding,
we awaken, beginning us
on an unending journey
toward enlightenment.

When the Wind Blows

The wind may be calm,
   gently blowing the
   leaves of trees, as they
   majestically sway in
   the soothing breeze.
It also may be fierce,
   causing enormous
   damage as storms emerge
   across our planet.
Just as the wind gusts,
   we often have moments
   in life affecting how
   intense our stress
   and emotions are.
In times of balance,
   we are steady.
There are periods in
   our lives, however, our
   reactions may be extreme.
When these occur, no
   longer in control, we
   may act out, harming
   others with our words,
   actions, or deeds.
To calm the winds, we
   must begin to understand
   there is another force
   active in our life
   besides the wind; it
   is the spirit, a piece

of god present
within every life.
With this realization,
we awaken.
With the acceptance
and guidance of our
spirit's inherent wisdom
and unconditional loving
beliefs, the wind calms,
enabling us to journey
further in our quest to
discover our genuine
purpose in life.

I Am Human

There are those who
believe the lives of
human beings are more
important than other
forms of life, and that
some people, due to
their differences, are
better than others.
Some embrace our
differences to justify
their beliefs and actions.
In reality, though we
may believe, look, act
differently, or we may
be a different genus,
we each possess a piece
of the divine within,
inextricably connecting
each of us to the other.
We have never been
greater or our lives
more significant than
anyone else or any other
life form; each possesses
a spirit, a piece of
god within as well.
Understanding this,
sharing our spirit's
inherent wisdom and
unconditional love to

selflessly help others
in need, is the lesson
we are alive to learn.

The Answers

The ego, our self-
  centered beliefs,
  tells us everything
  we need can be
  found in the world.
  If we even partially
  believe this, though
  we may have awoken,
  sensing the first
  messages from our
  spirit, enlightenment
  will remain elusive.
  The spirit, however,
  asks us to seek our
  answers within, where
  they have always been,
  and then to selflessly
  share the wisdom and
  unconditional love present
  there with all others.
  It is ironic, most spend
  their entire life searching
  for meaning in the
  world; it may not
  be found there.
  We have always
  had the answers.
  We were simply looking for
  them in the wrong place.
  We only had to open our

hearts, listen to the quiet
loving messages of our
spirit within, and we would
have understood this.

Here Comes the Sun

Over the nearby snow-
   covered mountain peaks,
   the first rays of the sun
   bring light and warmth
   to an indifferent self-
   centered world.
   It shines its light on all
   living things in its
   proximity, bringing hope
   to those who value its purpose.
   It does not discriminate
   on who receives its gifts,
   presenting its light to help
   plants and animals thrive
   and warmth to benefit
   all living things on
   our fragile world.
   We are the sun.
   With our warmth and
   light, we may each
   change the world by
   selflessly sharing our
   radiance and unconditional
   love to improve the
   lives of all.

Listen to the Silence

We all wish to be heard;
    it is part of being human.
    Yet it is not what we
    say that is important.
    Rather, it is what we hear
    when we genuinely listen
    to the messages behind
    the words being said.
    If we listen intently, we
    may hear the underlying
    meaning, hidden deep
    within the realm of
    the subconscious,
    not disguised by our
    self-centered opinions.
    If we remain quiet, we
    may hear the authentic
    messages of the spirit,
    accompanying each on
    their life's journey.
    It is a message of
    unconditional love,
    hope, and sincere desire
    for us to hear the
    messages from our
    own spirit as well.

Life Lessons

During our lives we
learn many lessons
about life that influence
our decisions and the
path we will take as we
strive to be happy,
successful, and live
a meaningful life.
If our experiences and
choices reinforce our
self-centered desire to
do only what is best for
ourself, then our goals in
life will never be realized.
Happiness, success, and
meaning may not be found
in a self-centered world.
They must first be
discovered within,
then selflessly shared,
without reservation,
with all others.
Only then will we not
only find what we desire,
but also discover the lesson
we are here to learn, the true
purpose of our life's journey.

Which Path Will We Follow?

There are but two
    paths through life
    we each may pursue.
    We may either follow
    the self-centered path
    of the ego, our learned
    beliefs; or we may seek
    the spiritual path, the
    one we were always
    meant to follow.
    The former idolizes money.
    Its primary concern is for
    our individual success in
    life, often defined by
    material possessions
    and other things we
    were told would make
    our lives worthwhile.
    Those pursuing a
    spiritual path, however,
    though they may have
    little money or possessions,
    are equally concerned about
    every life and how they
    may sincerely help others.
    We each choose which
    path through life to
    follow; we may change
    our path at any time.
    One path may lead to

success in the world,
though to leading a
life lacking meaning.
The other, though not
outwardly successful,
will lead to true inner
peace, happiness, love,
and discovering the
genuine purpose for
our life's journey.

Fear

Though fear may be
inherent, such as our
fight or flight reaction
to danger, there is also
acquired fear we learn
and worry about as
we are brought up
to be afraid of others.
This fear often is the
underlying cause of hate,
prejudice, war, and most
other negative emotions.
It results in a world of
needless death, hunger,
inequity, and numerous
unnecessary struggles by
many throughout history.
Only by selflessly
embracing love rather
than fear, accepting the
inherent good within
every life, will we be
able to break this
relentless cycle,
allowing our children
to live in a world of
peace rather than conflict.

Hiding From Pain

Many choose to hide
    from the hardships of
    life we each must confront.
    They may wear a mask,
    metaphorically covering
    their face to hide their
    true feelings and
    emotions from others.
    They may also conceal
    themselves behind a wall
    they erected within to
    protect them from the
    pain of living in a harsh
    often cruel world, where
    words, deeds, and
    actions, may cause
    stress, anxiety, and despair.
    In addition to the mask
    and wall, some may take
    drugs, drink alcohol, or
    find other ways to hide
    their authentic-self,
    from the world.
    Living like this isolates
    us not only from our
    acquaintances, but from
    friends, close family,
    and even ourselves.
    Though we may be
    surrounded by many

others, we are truly
alone, hiding from the
world, isolating who we
really are from all others.
We are each spirit.
The rest is simply an
illusion created by the
ego, our learned beliefs,
to help disguise our
genuine purpose in life.
It is only when we decide
to stop hiding, may we
finally find what we have
sought our entire lives:
happiness, unconditional
love, inner peace, and a
genuine understanding
of our life's true purpose.

The Rain

The rain is gently
   falling on an overcast
   cloudy day.
   Each drop splashes
   as it reaches the ground,
   helping nourish the
   earth and provide water
   to all who live on it.
   Though a single raindrop
   helps to slightly replenish
   the rivers and quench the
   thirst of one, alone it cannot
   sustain life by itself.
   Only combined with other
   raindrops, will it be able to
   satisfy the needs of many.
   We each are like a
   single raindrop.
   Alone, we are isolated,
   struggling to survive in
   a self-centered world.
   Together, however,
   selflessly helping each
   other, the needs of all
   may be met, allowing
   each to not only endure,
   but thrive as well.

Wealth

Many believe wealth is
having a lot of money,
material possessions,
being able to do the
best things life offers.
Though having these
make life easier, in truth,
wealth has little to do
with any of them.
This belief is an illusion
we accepted as real when
we were taught what
success and wealth are
in a self-centered world.
Real wealth comes from
within, and is only acquired
when we selflessly share
the wisdom and
unconditional
love of our spirit
with all others.
With this understanding
of what true wealth is,
our riches will be unearthed,
as we experience genuine
love, inner peace, and
discover the true
meaning of life.

Living in a Bubble

While we mature
　　within our mother,
　　we are enclosed in
　　an amniotic sac to
　　protect and provide
　　nourishment to us
　　until we are ready to
　　enter the world.
　　With our birth, no longer
　　requiring its help,
　　it is discarded.
　　It does not take long,
　　though, for another sac
　　to form, a bubble around
　　us, protecting us from
　　emotional pain and
　　nourishing our self-esteem.
　　This bubble is the ego,
　　our learned beliefs, and
　　it is reinforced by our
　　socialization into a self-
　　centered world.
　　Though this bubble
　　defends and nurtures us,
　　it also isolates us from
　　each other and from
　　our authentic-self.
　　As long as the bubble is
　　intact, even if its walls
　　are thin, we will continue

to struggle to find
meaning in our lives.
It is only when we burst
the bubble, as we once
did upon our birth, we
may begin a quest to
discover our true
purpose in life.

Building a Wall or a Bridge

In life, we may choose
    whether to build a
    wall or a bridge.
    The wall isolates us
    from not only each
    other, but from
    ourself as well.
    It hides the beauty in
    the distance of faraway
    mountain tops, meandering
    rivers, and open meadows
    full of flowers.
    Instead we find a barrier
    we cannot see through,
    blocking our view of
    the world's grandeur.
    The bridge is quite different.
    Rather than dividing us,
    it connects all life
    to each other.
    In the distance, the views
    remain unobstructed as
    we are able to see through
    it to the other side.
    If we view the world
    through a wall, having
    only a partial view of it
    as we peer over the
    top, we will only see
    a superficial image, a

façade, we each
project to others.
When we see a world
full of bridges though,
instead of walls, we see
kindness, unconditional
love, present within
every life, desiring only
to selflessly help all others.
To change the future and
further the spiritual
evolution of our planet,
we must tear down all
our isolating walls,
replacing them instead
with bridges that will
connect us all together.

The Will of God

God is known by
    many names.
    Spirit, soul, higher-self,
    are but three spiritual names
    synonymous with god.
    Allah, Jehovah, Yahweh,
    are also known as god in
    three prominent world religions.
    Though many know god
    by different names, god
    has only one underlying
    message uniting each:
    sharing unconditional
    love with all.
    The will of god does not
    tolerate hate, intolerance,
    self-centered greed.
    Nor does it condone
    allowing needless
    death due to starvation,
    war, indifference.
    Or the struggles of so
    many due to poverty,
    homelessness, prejudice.
    God is love.
    Believing in god means
    equally sharing and
    selflessly helping
    everyone, regardless
    of our differences, and

treating all other forms
of life and mother earth
with the respect she deserves.
This is the will of god.
Anything else is a learned
illusion, propagated by
organized religion, that
long ago lost sight of
the true meaning and
beliefs god intended.

A Candle in the Wind

A calm breeze gently
    blows the flame of a
    candle flickering its
    light and warmth on
    all surrounding it.
    The candle connects
    each together with
    its mystifying glow.
    We are all candles in
    the wind, intimately
    connected by a universal
    spirit, uniting us as one
    in our brief journey
    through life.
    Only by selflessly
    helping each other
    will our light become
    brighter and our life
    more meaningful.

The Eyes of a Spirit

A spirit, a piece
of god dwells
within every life.
It views the world
with unconditional
love, meant to be
selflessly shared
with all others.
There are no
alternative motives
or emotions.
The eyes of a spirit
see beyond the façade
others project, directly
hearing the messages of
the other's spirit within.
When we are attentive
to our spirit, we sense
the true meaning of
another, as it effortlessly
communicates silently with
the other's divine presence.
To really know another,
be silent, listen quietly
to the genuine meaning
you sense in between
your racing thoughts.
It is only then you will
know what they are truly saying.

Some Days We Eat

I am four years old today.
    Though it is my birthday,
    my family cannot afford
    to buy me a cake or presents.
    We are quite poor, do not
    have a home to live in
    or warm clothes to wear.
    Many days we do not
    have any food to eat
    either, though my parents
    try to earn money.
    We are homeless; I
    am always afraid.
    Some days, I walk past
    others like us, who died
    during the night from
    sickness, lack of food,
    or being hurt by someone else.
    I wonder why our family
    and others have to
    live like this.
    I dream to be like other
    children who have a home,
    food to eat every day,
    clothes to wear that
    keep them warm.
    I do not understand why
    they do not help us and
    others like us who
    are not as fortunate.

Are these people
better than us?
Are their lives more
important because they
have more money?
I do not believe they are.
If I were in charge of
the world, everyone
would share what they
have so no one would
need to struggle as we are.
This is the world we
live in, though it does
not need to be.
We are meant selflessly
share our wealth and
excess, allowing everyone,
regardless of our differences
or accomplishments, to be
helped in their time of need,
so no one needlessly suffers.
This is the spiritual path
through life we were
always meant to follow.
This is the lesson we
are here to learn.

Darkness and Light

Darkness is not within.
    It comes from the self-
    centered world around
    us and is internalized.
    Within there is only light.
    Darkness, learned after
    we are born, dominates
    the views and actions of
    most, causing many of
    the man-made problems
    in the world.
    Though darkness will
    always remain throughout
    our life, it need not
    control our choices.
    It is only when we
    allow light to direct
    our actions, becoming
    our primary guide in life,
    the world may finally
    evolve, allowing our
    children to grow up in
    a world of peace rather
    than war, tolerance
    rather than prejudice,
    and love rather than hate.

We Are God

If there is a definition
    of god, it would be
    the totality of all
    spirits connected to
    each other by their
    proximity and,
    therefore, existing
    as one entity.
    This one entity,
    present in an alternate
    plane of existence at a
    higher vibrational level,
    may be considered to be god.
    To take this discussion one
    step further, every spirit
    would therefore represent
    a piece or part of god.
    Since there is a spirit
    within everyone and
    everything alive, there
    is a part or piece of
    god within every
    life as well.

Look Beyond the Façade

When you see someone,
    look beyond the façade.
    See the good within; the
    pretense is not real.
    It is a fiction created
    by the ego, our learned
    beliefs, from everything
    we have learned and
    accepted as true
    in our life.
    Despite our
    accomplishments
    or differences,
    every life is equally
    valuable, intimately
    connected by a
    universal spirit within.
    To truly know another,
    see the genuine soul within.

When Children Start Dying

How can the
    senseless death of
    even one child be
    acceptable?
    Whether that child
    died in war, from
    starvation, a treatable
    illness, or in any other
    manner, their loss will
    be suffered by everyone;
    their essence within no
    longer present to shine
    their light on the world.
    This is true not only of
    children, but every
    life as well.
    Is someone's life,
    because of their wealth,
    fame, job, ethnicity, race,
    or any other comparison,
    more valuable than
    another's who is poor,
    homeless, a minority?
    If you answered yes,
    then you have found a
    way to rationalize
    our children dying.
    If you answered no
    though, perhaps it is
    time to awaken,

understanding every
life is, and always has
been, equally valuable
and those most
vulnerable, our children,
their light must never
again be allowed to
senselessly darken.

The Illusion

Life is an illusion,
    beginning when
    we are young, as
    we are taught how to
    survive in the world.
    We learn from every
    interaction we have
    in our daily lives.
    These ideas form the
    basis of the person we
    are to become, often for
    the remainder our life.
    The ego, our learned
    beliefs, teaches us to
    accept the self-centered
    status quo of the world
    in which we live.
    Those doing so, remain
    asleep, living in a
    world of deception.
    With enlightenment,
    the illusions we were
    taught and accepted
    as real are exposed.
    The egocentric world
    of the matrix dissolves,
    truth in its wake.
    Little we learned
    in life was true.
    Truth may not be

discovered in a self-
centered world.
It only lies within, where
it has always been.
Then, it must be
selflessly shared with
others to help them
discover truth in
their life as well.

The Elder

With age, the
   inevitability of
   death creeps closer.
   Now, considered elders
   in society, many review
   the life they had lived.
   Material possessions,
   prestige, beliefs, wealth,
   begin to have less meaning.
   Those who have lived a
   successful life are not
   immune to this review;
   death does not favor them.
   At this time, some may
   finally begin to understand
   their definition of success
   may have been flawed.
   Achieving success in the
   world to only benefit
   ourselves has not made
   their lives meaningful
   or important.
   In fact, they may start
   to realize the exact
   opposite is true.
   The elder may begin
   to sense a message
   within telling them
   true success in life may
   only be experienced by

selflessly helping others
become successful in
their life as well.

Thoughts and Prayers

After a preventable
    tragedy, observing
    children and others
    dying from senseless
    violence, how many
    more times must we
    hear "our thoughts and
    prayers are with
    those who died."
    These heartbreaking
    deaths are avoidable,
    caused the greed and
    desire for power of the
    few and the acceptance
    by the rest of the status quo.
    Any law or action taken
    should have only one
    underlying consideration;
    what is best for everyone,
    not just the select few.
    Every life is equally important.
    It matters not our race,
    wealth, beliefs or any
    other comparison we
    may make; each deserves
    to be treated with respect
    and unconditional love,
    helped in their time of need.
    Only when this is
    finally realized and

accepted will thoughts
and prayers for avertable
tragedies no longer be
necessary, and the
spiritual evolution of
humanity become reality.

Emotions

After we are born
    we learn what happiness,
    love, and other emotions
    are by observing
    those around us.
    Though we may
    believe we understand
    what they are, we do not.
    Learned emotions are
    conditional, often
    reflected by our own
    desires and needs.
    Only unconditional
    emotions, inherent
    within each life,
    selflessly shared
    without pause or
    benefit, are genuine.
    To truly know
    another, gaze deeply
    within their soul,
    where these dormant
    emotions, long hidden
    from view, have
    always been.

Waking Up From A Dream

Many go through
    life asleep, living in
    a twilight fog cloaking
    their vision of life.
    Those living like this,
    believe and accept
    everything they learned
    about life was true.
    Despite their success
    in the world though,
    there may come a time
    in their life they begin
    to question if what
    they learned was true.
    A feeling deep within,
    begins to emerge
    wondering if there is
    more to life than success.
    At this point, they
    begin to awaken from
    their lifelong slumber,
    arousing them from
    their dream, beginning
    them on an enduring
    journey toward enlightenment.

Spiritual Karma

There are those who
appear to evade justice,
committing deeds
harming others to
benefit themselves.
Though this may allow
them to be successful,
wealthy, powerful, it
does not allow them
to escape judgement.
Those who hurt others
in anyway, though they
may appear not to suffer
any consequences, having
achieved success in the
world, will never find
true happiness, love,
or meaning in their life.
As they approach death,
reviewing their life,
they will experience
the pain they caused to
every person throughout
their life and will then
realize, their life,
though successful, was led
without meaning or purpose.

The Eyes of a Child

When a child is born
and see the world for
the first time, their
eyes are wide open.
They know only one
emotion: unconditional
love meant to be shared
with all others.
From that very moment
though, when the child's
view of the world is
crystal clear, their eyes
begin to close, as they
are taught what to
believe in the self-
centered world they
are to live in.
The more the child
accepts what they learn,
the further their eyes
will close to the true
possibilities life offers.
There are some who
are blind; others who
must wear aids to
help them see.
The only thing in life
that is authentic is
unconditional love;
everything else is

an illusion.
When we truly
understand this,
we will be able to
fully reopen our
eyes once more,
as they were when
we were first born.

Which Way is the Wind Blowing?

Throughout our lives,
    the wind gusts may
    determine how
    challenging our
    life will be.
    We discover our lives
    are easiest when the
    wind is blowing behind
    us, allowing us to
    effortlessly move forward.
    When this happens, we
    settle into a pattern
    repeating our daily
    routine, trying to enjoy
    the benefits life brings.
    We are content accepting
    the status quo, believing
    all we were taught is true.
    As we approach death,
    though we may have
    had a good job, made
    a lot of money, had a
    family, and many material
    possessions, when we
    review our lives, we
    may wonder where
    the years have gone,
    if our life truly
    had meaning.
    It is then we may

finally understand,
it did not.
Though it is much
more difficult, it is
only when we decide
to walk against the
wind, being equally
concerned for every
life, rather than only
our own, will we
discover the genuine
reason for our
life's journey.

Don't Follow the Crowd

From our first breath
   we are taught to conform
   to the beliefs of others.
   We are told to only worry
   and be concerned for
   ourself as we learn
   how to survive in a
   self-centered world.
   Though there are
   some who are taught
   about god through
   their religious practices,
   what they learned from
   organized religion was
   corrupted by man's
   interpretation long ago.
   Those who are
   indoctrinated into
   the world like this,
   follow the crowd,
   doing what is expected
   of them to live a
   successful life.
   By following the
   status quo, though
   they may appear to
   have led a good life,
   they will have ignored
   the lessons they
   were born to learn.

Only when we no
longer follow the
crowd, realizing
little we were taught
was true, designed
to have us follow
a false path through
life, may we begin a
quest to discover the
genuine reason for
our life's journey.

About Ken

Peace, Love, & Light

My name is Ken Luball ~ Spiritual ~ Seeker ~ Author ~ Guide ~

****

Ever since I was a young child, I knew my purpose in life; it was for me to awaken, find enlightenment, and share my experience and knowledge with others. To reach those lofty aspirations though, I first had to navigate through quite a few unexpected detours in my life. Though I was brought up in a religious family, it did not help me hear the messages from my spirit guide, Bodhi. If anything, religion only further isolated me, teaching me to accept the ego's view of religion rather than Bodhi's. It was not until after I stopped following a formal religion, I finally was able to embrace spirituality, and with this embrace, I awoke.

Spirituality is the belief there is a piece of god, a spirit, within everything that has life, and, because of this, all life is important, equal, and connected. After I awoke, no longer having the dogma of religion handicapping my views, I was suddenly free to explore this philosophy of life more deeply. Only then did I become aware of the mask I wore and the impenetrable wall I had erected around my heart; the mask and wall allowed me to survive in the world. I would always smile, appear happy, though I would often feel intense anxiety within. This was something I never really understood until the moment I confronted my ego. Little did I know these survival mechanisms would have a profound effect on me for the majority of my life. By protecting me from emotional pain, they also isolated me from my family, everyone else in my life, and even from myself. No one could hurt me because I did not allow anyone to get close enough to do so. In turn, no one could love me or was I able to truly love another either. This superficial life, one devoid of risk or pain, left me alone in a sea of people.

It took many years before the first cracks in my wall formed and before I could loosen the mask I constantly wore. It took me almost an entire lifetime to awaken and begin my journey toward enlightenment.

After I was clearly able to hear my spirit guide, Bodhi, I realized everything I had learned from my ego throughout my life was untrue. I had looked for love and happiness in the job I had, the money I made, things I owned, and through my wife and children. With the exception of the latter, I finally realized none of those things truly mattered. This does not mean I am ungrateful to my ego, however. It taught me coping skills and allowed me to succeed, or at least what I thought success was. Though my ego still remains with me, it has taken a more secondary role in my life now, relinquishing its former primary role to my spirit guide, Bodhi.

Decisions were now required. While it was tempting to take this newly found state of being, withdraw from society and all the hate, fear, cruelty, poverty, and greed that plagues it, I knew within myself, this knowledge was to be shared with others. That is my destiny. Therefore, I have written A Mystical Trilogy: '*Our Search for Meaning*': a series of three books of thoughtful easily understandable spiritual reflections about life; A Spiritual Duology: '*Spiritual Reflections*': two books of spiritual reflections using metaphor, imagery, and spiritual insight to explore themes of awakening, enlightenment, and the human pursuit of meaning; and *The Awakening Tetralogy* : the first three stories in *The Awakening Tetralogy* follow the spiritual journey through life of a child, as they learn the lessons needed during their life to awaken and become enlightened. It is my hope you will read these books, and in doing so, begin a new adventure;

one where you will awaken and further your journey toward enlightenment with your spirit within.

I do not know if these books will be widely read in my lifetime, though I hope one day they may help others awaken and find enlightenment as well.

"We are all on a spiritual journey of love & peace;
together may we spread light throughout the world."

To read more of Ken's life-changing reflections visit his website:
kenluball.com[2]

~ ~

Also by Ken Luball

"The Awakening Tetralogy" - A Series of Four Spiritual Books
Today I Am Going to Die: Choices in Life
The Spirit Guide: Journey Through Life
Tranquility: A Village of Hope
The Illusion of Happiness: Choosing Love Over Fear

Watch for more at kenluball.com.

About the Author

My name is Ken Luball. Spiritual Seeker ~ Author ~ Guide. ** Author of "The Awakening Tetralogy: A series of Four Spiritual Books". **

Ever since I was a young child, I knew my purpose in life; it was to Awaken, find Enlightenment, and share my experience and knowledge with others. To reach those lofty aspirations though, I first had to navigate through quite a few unexpected detours in my life. It was not until after I stopped following a formal religion, I finally was able to embrace *Spirituality*, and with this embrace, I *Awoke*.

Spirituality is the belief there is a piece of God (a *Spirit*) within everything that has life, and, because of this, all life is important, equal, and connected.

It took me almost an entire lifetime to become to be *Awakened* and begin my journey towards *Enlightenment.*

After I Awoke I realized everything I had *Learned* throughout my life was untrue. I had looked for love and happiness in the job I had, the money I made, things I owned, and through my wife and children. With the exception of the latter, I finally realized none of those things truly mattered.

I knew Enlightenment was a gift to be shared with others. That is my destiny. Therefore, I have written "The Awakening Tetralogy", a series of four "Spiritual" books. It is my hope by reading these books, you will begin a new adventure. One where you will *Awaken* and further your journey towards *Enlightenment* with your Spirit Within.

Read more at kenluball.com.